VENUSBERG

BOOKS BY
ANTHONY POWELL

NOVELS
Afternoon Men
Venusberg
From a View to a Death
Agents and Patients
What's Become of Waring

A DANCE TO THE MUSIC OF TIME
A Question of Upbringing
A Buyer's Market
The Acceptance World
At Lady Molly's
Casanova's Chinese Restaurant
The Kindly Ones
The Valley of Bones
The Soldier's Art
The Military Philosophers
Books Do Furnish a Room
Temporary Kings

GENERAL
John Aubrey and his Friends

PLAYS
The Garden God and *The Rest I'll Whistle*

VENUSBERG

by

ANTHONY POWELL

HEINEMANN : LONDON

William Heinemann Ltd
15 Queen Street, Mayfair, London W1X 8BE

LONDON MELBOURNE TORONTO
JOHANNESBURG AUCKLAND

First published 1932 (Duckworth)
New edition 1955 (Heinemann)
Reprinted 1962, 1967, 1974

434 59913 1

0999 290 738

Printed in Great Britain by
REDWOOD BURN LIMITED
Trowbridge & Esher

'Here, according to popular tradition, is situated the grotto of Venus, into which she enticed the knight Tannhäuser; fine view from the top.'

I

LUSHINGTON collected the pieces of typewritten foolscap and shook them together so that the edges were level. Outside, it was raining. The literary editor said:

'Seeing the world broadens the outlook. You can learn a lot abroad. They're a funny lot, foreigners. I always go abroad for my holiday. I like it over there. The food makes a change. I shouldn't wonder if it wasn't pretty cold where you're going. Still, I expect you'll be sorry to leave old London all the same. We have some fun here when we do. I don't know any town like it. I don't really.'

The literary editor took out his penknife and, breathing hard, trimmed where his thumbnail had a jagged edge. Lushington opened a box of paper clips and took one out. He pressed the paper clip through the corner of the sheets of foolscap upon which he had begun an article, and put them into a small dispatch-case. The literary editor finished off the nail by biting it, shut the penknife and put it back into his pocket. Miss Arnold said:

'I expect you'll give up newspaper work when you get out there, Mr. Lushington, and go into business and become a millionaire. All the best men become foreign correspondents for a bit. They say there is nothing like abroad for training.'

The literary editor said: 'They've taken the place of the old diplomat. Better educated. Better informed. Better paid. And, of course, more reliable. But they carry on the same fine tradition.'

Lushington said: 'Well, you will remember about trying to use both those two stories of mine for the feature page, won't you? It would be a great help if you could. I'd be very grateful.'

'I'll have a look at them just as soon as I have a moment to spare, which ought to be some time the day after to-morrow.'

Lushington shut the dispatch-case and picked up his hat. Water dripped down the outer panes of the windows, one of which rattled three times at regular intervals. Outside, it was winter. Miss Arnold said:

'Well, good-night, Mr. Lushington, and good luck.'

The literary editor said: 'So long, Lushington, and all the best, and don't forget to put that dope in the post tonight so that Booth gets it in time for the woman's page.'

Taking the dispatch-case and pondering in his mind whether he would go home and finish the article and go to bed, or call on Lucy and sit up all night and finish the article, Lushington went down the stairs, which were of stone like those of a prison or lunatic asylum and were, in effect, used to some considerable extent by persons of a criminal tendency or mentally deranged. In the atmosphere there was a smell of icy damp paint permeating the rawness of the night. The wind circulated through the corridors and up and down the lift-shaft. He walked down several flights of stairs wondering whether he had remembered to pack his evening shoes. At the entrance the man with the birth-mark on his face who sat at a desk in a cubicle and asked people their names and controlled the house telephone without much success said:

'So you're saying ta-ta to us all for a bit?'

'That's it.'

Shaken by a fit of coughing, a bronchial upheaval like a tornado in its suddenness, the man said:

'Grand weather for travelling, I don't think.'

He struck himself several times on the chest and then spat through the door of the wooden cubicle in which he was confined, neatly, and far out into the corner of the passage.

'That's a nasty cough of yours,' Lushington said.

'Rise and fall of the leaf finds out them with weak chests.'

'It sure does.'

'Suffered from asthma since I was a little kid not so high.'

'You have?'

The man passed his hand lightly over his birthmark and said:

'It's the truth. Well, I hope it keeps fine for you.'

'And *I*,' said Lushington, 'hope it keeps fine for *you*.'

He went into the street, where it was raining and cold. The lights disappeared suddenly in the windows of the pub on the other side of the road and deciding in favour of Lucy he got into a bus. Inside he tried to think of a joke to round off the article with. The bus bumped along through the rain. No joke quickened within him. It was too cold a night for that sort of joke, one of the good universal kind.

Coming of that professional stock who, like the Jews, live secretly, holding at intervals well-attended family conclaves, remaining securely out of touch with life, Lushington had begun his career in the City. An almost absolute business inability and perhaps some hereditary flaw in his character had led him to journalism, and being ambitious he hoped one of these days to become dramatic critic on a paper with a decent circulation. Meanwhile he was going as special correspondent to a country on the Baltic, the name of which he could never remember. He was a serious young man with a pink and white face who believed implicitly in eventual progress on a scientific basis, although he had had Anglo-Catholic leanings in his City days.

3

There was nothing at all extraordinary in Lushington's appointment to this post. It was the sort of thing that happened every day. More than this, it had been what he had wanted not so long before and was to some extent the delayed action of past intriguing. He was, in short, as the literary editor had said, lucky to get it. But there was a circumstance that gave the appointment some of the tang of a stale joke, a flavour used-up but at the same time forceful and disturbing like a tune running tiresomely in his head. This significance consisted in Da Costa being honorary attaché at the legation of that same Baltic state. Da Costa was not only an old friend of Lushington. He was also the man with whom Lucy was in love. Lushington could not therefore avoid reflecting, on hearing of his good fortune, that he was both leaving Lucy and going to a place where he would be reminded perpetually of her feelings for Da Costa.

Lushington and Da Costa had been at school together. Da Costa's setting was similar to Lushington's without being precisely the same. He came of a large and moderately influential family whose possibly Iberian ancestors had made money in India, nabobs under the Regency, who, marrying with discernment, had formed a vaguely empire-building tradition. Da Costa himself did not belong to this tradition. It embarrassed him a little. But now in the last resort he had found himself unable to circumvent it. After coming down from Oxford he had hung about, working at a thesis on comparative religion. And then Lushington had introduced him to Lucy and the trouble had begun.

Da Costa like Lushington was shy. But whereas Lushington's shyness took the form of creeping about rooms pretending that he was really not there at all, Da Costa's manifested itself in shouting loud and laughing and upsetting things to counteract this feeling of personal inadequacy. As it happened, Da Costa was good at games and examinations, so that his difficulties were pretty fundamental ones and not merely adolescent non-adaptability setbacks. For example, unlike Lushington he was bored by the society of women. He could stand them only for an hour or so on end. This was due to an unusual mental orientation, or perhaps to laziness because he was not prepared to concede the exactions of time and energy that prolonged intimacy with one would require. In some ways, they attracted him to a considerable extent and once he had been induced by friends to spend a week-end with an intellectually cultured chorus girl. It was not, however, a success and in any case, as Da Costa himself used to point out, he had not enough money to prolong the relationship. Then for a short time he was always seen about with a major's widow. But it did not do. There was something, as his friends used to say, lacking. In spite of this and perhaps because of it women liked him. Among them Lucy.

Lushington had met Lucy at the house of the man who wrote the music column for his paper. Nothing had marked their meeting as in any way out of the ordinary. Lushington liked her, but it was not until several weeks after this first meeting that he fell in love with her and it was some months later before he had the courage to tell her so. He had never been in love before, except slightly with one of his first cousins, who was already engaged to a man in the Treasury, and he was surprised when he found that Lucy returned his feelings. He was not at all certain what he ought to do.

In due course she became his mistress. She was not a vicious girl, but she had had two husbands and had become accustomed to doing as she wished. But all the time she knew that he was not what she was looking for. That was one of the reasons why she would not marry him. Lushing-

5

ton on his side, surprised when he found that Lucy was attracted by him, was amazed when he found himself living with her, and before he had begun to consider their relationship as anything less than a phenomenon he had lost her by introducing her to Da Costa just at the moment when he was beginning to feel that she really belonged to himself. He lost her in the sense that she gave him up as a lover. His place was not taken by Da Costa, because Da Costa was for a long time unaware how matters stood and even when he became aware took no steps in the matter. Something about his unbalanced manner and respectable background had appealed at once to Lucy, but he felt towards her, as towards most of the women whom he met, only an amiable lack of interest. However, it flattered him at first that he should have made such an impression on her, and then annoyed him when he found that he had caused a great deal of unnecessary trouble and had gained one of those emotional responsibilities which he devoted so much of his time to avoiding.

For a short time the situation had adjusted itself by all three of them going about a great deal together, because they liked each other's company and this system enabled Lushington to be with Lucy and Lucy to be with Da Costa. It was a working compromise but it got on everybody's nerves. In the end it was Da Costa who decided that he could stand it no more. He decided to leave England and his family, who had repeatedly requested in the past that he should do something useful, but suggested that he should join the legation of a relative who was Minister at this obscurely northern capital. The idea was fostered by his elder brother, who was married and had several children and who had once been called the most popular man in Throgmorton Street. The post of honorary attaché was considered by the Da Costa family to be the very thing.

Da Costa himself liked the idea because, being a young man with wide interests, he wanted to see abroad and, although he was unsatisfactory as an attaché, he himself found congenial the purely formal social contacts of his profession, which was in this respect a great improvement upon what he had been accustomed to in London. His relative, as it happened, retired soon after his arrival, but this was due to a personal whim and was unconnected with Da Costa's shortcomings. In the meanwhile a new Minister had not yet been appointed, and as the routine work at the legation had to be completed somehow, the *chargé d'affaires* made no effort to eject Da Costa during the interregnum.

And now Lushington's newspaper had decided to send him to the same place. He was to stay there for some months and write about the political situations. Undeniably it was a good job. But at the same time there were drawbacks.

2

THE bus stopped and Lushington got out and went through the passage with posts across it which led to the square where Lucy lived. The rain was falling in a measured way on the leaves of the trees inside the square's railings. He rang the bell. Then he waited, listening to the rain and the noise of the water running down the wall of the next house where one of the outside gutters had burst. Lucy opened the door herself. She was wearing a dressing-gown over her pyjamas and said:

'Oh it's you, is it? Come in, sweet, but I'm afraid there isn't such a thing as a cigarette in the house.'

'Why are you dressed like this? Are you ill?'

'I'm just going to bed. I'm going to have a bath and then go to bed. Why have you come to see me now?'

She was fair and had short curly hair and she held the dressing-gown tight across her body so that it showed her figure and her round, knowing, little breasts. He went through the door and followed her into the sitting-room. She slipped her arm through his and into the pocket of his overcoat, taking his hand. Lushington put his hat on the table. Then he kissed Lucy.

'Why have you come now?' she said.

She finished kissing him and went away and lay down on the sofa, under a tartan rug, turning sideways and resting her head on the end of the sofa. Lushington took off his overcoat and sat down in one of the arm-chairs. He said:

8

'It's settled that I go tomorrow.'

'By train?'

'By boat. I thought I might make a story of it for the paper.'

'Are you glad to be going?'

'I don't mind much either way.'

'Why aren't you glad?'

'Well, I shan't be seeing you for some time.'

'You must find someone else,' she said. 'You must really. You can't go on like this. It's absurd. Besides, it's awful for me. Can't you find someone else?'

'Perhaps I will out there.'

'It's funny you're going to the same place.'

'It's in the news, you see. They've been having political troubles. Revolutions and so on. Front page stuff, almost.'

'Don't go and get shot.'

'I expect I shall.'

'It's a pity I can't come with you.'

'Yes, why don't you?'

She pulled the rug almost over her head and turned away from him towards the inside of the sofa, doubling herself up. There was a pause. She lay there looking a little like a sick child, very slight and taking up hardly any room on the sofa. Outside, the rain came thudding against the window. Lushington said:

'You haven't told me why you are dressed like that yet.'

'I'm not well. I'm going to have a bath and go to bed.'

'What's wrong with you?'

'I don't know,' she said, 'I'm just not well. I haven't been well for weeks. I hate everything. That's why I'm not well. There is nothing to be done about it. But tell me about yourself. What has been happening? Anything?'

'Nothing much. Except that I'm going away. And I've told you that.'

'Who was that with you when I saw you the other night? In green?'

'I don't think you know her. I met her somewhere. She looks rather nice, don't you think?'

'I hate those slit eyes. You're not in love with her or anything like that, are you? I don't trust your taste.'

'No, I'm not.'

Lucy laughed and threw the rug on the floor and stretched out her arms. Then she stood up, still laughing. She said:

'Anyway I suppose I ought to have my bath now.'

'Do you mind if I finish off an article on your typewriter?' Lushington said.

'There's paper in the drawer.'

'Here?'

'Yes.'

He watched her go into the bathroom, a narrow den leading out of the sitting-room, and heard her turn on the geyser. He sat for a few moments in front of the typewriter thinking of the first time he had seen her.

At seventeen Lucy had run away with her first husband, who was rumoured once to have held a war-time commission in a Guards battalion. Her father, a captain retired from the Marines, who had lost his wife's money by judicious investments, lived in a bungalow on the south coast with his eight children and this used sometimes to make him appear a discontented man. But his wife was a woman who looked always on the bright side, so that in later life Lucy used to say that she could never remember which of her parents had contributed most towards her elopement. Lucy had been married at Torquay and her husband had worn an Old Etonian tie which he had seen on his way there in a glass case on Paddington station. But although he had initiative he was an ignorant and rather greedy man and the marriage had lasted less than eighteen months.

Not long after the decree was made absolute it became apparent that she was more than remarkably good-looking. She showed signs of becoming a film star. But she was a girl who felt that life should be full of meaning and she broke with her second husband, a film producer, because he adapted one of the minor classics too freely. After that she lived on alimony and occasionally had lovers. But somehow it was not a success although as a sex she liked men, and in the evening she used to sit in her room and play the gramophone or read a book because, although this was not very amusing, it seemed better than going about with the people who were her friends. She often said so. She often told Lushington when he became her lover that she felt like this. Also it filled up the time while she waited for the ideal man, who became as the months went on an increasingly improbable figure, because her adventures, particularly those on the films, had caused her to develop a mild but insidious megalomania. But even after she had decided that Da Costa was what she wanted Lushington used often to visit her because she could not have Da Costa, who was not interested in anyone at all.

Lushington opened the dispatch-case and put one of the sheets of paper into the machine. Lucy came out of the bathroom and watched him typing. Clouds of steam began to puff into the sitting-room. She took up the rug again and wrapping it round her knees sat on the edge of the sofa. Lushington typed. The article had to be finished somehow. The steam began to fill all one side of the room with fog. Lucy went into the bathroom again and, without shutting the door, turned off the water. He heard her get into the bath and begin to splash about. He wrote:

'. . . and, too, why do people keep on repeating the old,

11

old lie that the only maidens with sex-appeal are the ones who want always to be having a good time? When will all those would-be clever people commence to understand that that girl who holds our heart in thrall is the old-fashioned miss, whom our grandfather loved as she tripped demurely between rose-blossoms, along the garden path, in that quaint old-fashioned frock to meet her sweetheart. After all it is among the kindly, everyday folk that you find garnered-in the best hearts, among those worth-while, simple souls . . .'

He wrote for some time. Lucy splashed about next door. Outside a clock struck. It was still pouring with rain.

Lushington took the last sheet out of the typewriter and read it through, altering 'empirical' to 'real-life.' Then he lit a cigarette. From the bathroom Lucy said:

'It's a new country, isn't it?'

'Yes.'

'Who used to own it?'

'Russia. I think Germany had some of it too, I'm not sure.'

'Come and talk if you have finished.'

He clipped the sheets of paper together and put them once more into the dispatch-case. Then he went into the bathroom. Lucy was lying on her back, only her head appearing, the light deflected through the water making it join her shoulders obliquely as if it grew at a sharp angle to the rest of her body. Lushington said:

'I'm going now. Good-bye.'

'Don't go yet. Why go now? I've hardly seen you at all.'

'I've still got some packing to do.'

'You poor darling.'

She sat up in the bath and reached out for the towel to dry her hands and arms. Painfully he became aware of how lovely she was and how much he wanted her. For the moment he was glad even that he was going away where he would not see her, so that perhaps by being distant from her he might not want her so much. She threw away the towel and put her arms round his neck and he held the cigarette away at arm's length to keep the smoke from her face.

'Good-bye,' she said, 'I hope you have a lovely time.'

'What are you going to do?'

'I may be staying with people in the country for a bit.'

'At the home of that curious new admirer of yours?'

'I expect so.'

'Is he nice?'

'Yes,' she said, 'I'm very fond of him. He has very nice manners.'

'He has no roof to his mouth, has he?'

'The poor boy is very sweet really. He's so young.'

'Well, good-bye,' said Lushington, 'I'll write and tell you all about life out there. How we all are.'

'Thank you, darling.'

He stood there not wanting to go. She said suddenly:

'Do you think he's like that? Always has been? I mean is it really no good? Will it never be any good?'

'Who?'

'Him.'

'No, of course not. How absurd. He has had girls. Very dull ones, I admit. But women don't amuse him much.'

'He is undersexed?'

'He is not in the least undersexed. You think there is something pathological about every man who does not fall for you.'

'But he doesn't like women.'

'He gets on without them. Some men can. It has been done.'

'Then he is undersexed.'

'All right. He's undersexed.'

She said: 'Don't get angry. All I mean is do you think

that one of these days he might begin to like me?'

'I daresay.'

'Do you think so?'

'In the meantime please remember that there is always me.'

'Darling.'

He shut the door behind him and went down the stairs out into the square. The rain had stopped, but water still trickled down the wall of the house next door. A gramophone was playing in one of the basements as he passed and he stood for a few moments listening to it. The curtains did not meet across the windows of the room, so that he could see people inside who were dancing. He watched them for a time, oppressed by the recognition that there was still some packing to be done. Then he walked home, posting the article in the letter-box at the end of the square.

3

THE boat was small. It smelt of cocoanut oil and was to call at Copenhagen on the voyage. Recreation on board was limited to reading in a bunk or sitting in what was called the *smoke saloon* and talking to Count Scherbatcheff. It was also possible to talk to Count Scherbatcheff while walking up and down the deck, and this was in fact preferable when the two Danish young men from Manchester University who were interested in radio sat in the smoke saloon with their friend the German commercial traveller. Count Scherbatcheff, who was about thirty, had a fair moustache and, having studied engineering in Belgium, he sometimes wore a béret with three different-coloured buttons in it, each of which stood for something definite in his life. He and Lushington used to lean over the side of the boat and discuss expenses and similar matters.

The North Sea, an engrailed tract of sheet-iron, heaved a little. All the sky was grey. Count Scherbatcheff, who had stomach trouble of some sort, patted the front of his overcoat. He said:

'For example, my great-uncle was a very extravagant man. He used to have supper-parties after the opera. Very often at these parties he would give chorus girls baths of champagne. He would astonish gypsies and such people by his behaviour.'

'Often the only baths that they ever got?'

'I should not be surprised. Moreover in Russia before the Revolution we used to give huge tips. It was absurd. It was unnecessary. I can give you no idea how large they were. Really it was ridiculous. I can remember when I was a schoolboy going out to dinner by myself at Yalta and leaving the waiter an outrageously large tip. A great deal too much.'

Lushington turned up the collar of his overcoat. He hoped that it was not going to be rough. There was a red, weak sun but a cloud was reflected darkly in the metal surfaces of water. The boat heaved again. Count Scherbatcheff, steadying himself with a piece of rigging, said:

'It will be bad in the Baltic. There it will almost certainly be rough. In the Baltic the sea is often very stormy. I shall not be surprised if the weather is inclement on this trip.'

They walked up and down the deck. Sometimes other ships passed on the horizon. It appeared that Count Scherbatcheff was going on a visit to his grandmother, who disliked travelling and, when the Revolution came, had refused to emigrate as far as England or France.

'She is a woman of great obstinacy,' Count Scherbatcheff said. 'Like all my family she is very obstinate. I myself am very obstinate. It was for this reason that she refused to move.'

'Did she stay there during the Revolution and the War of Independence?'

'Through both. And through the civil war that followed them.'

'She was lucky to escape. How did she do it?'

'When the trouble began she had been staying with cousins who had a small estate in the neighbourhood. A house which afterwards was burned. We Russians are not popular with these people and especially this was so during the Revolution and before the Independence was declared. My grandmother was out walking one day when she was thrown from the Nikolai bridge by some members of the Social-Democratic party.'

'Into the river?'

'It was the custom. It was from the Nikolai bridge that Jews were sometimes thrown.'

'Why?'

'Jews. I cannot say the word. *Les Juifs*. It is hard to pronounce. *Jews*. That is how you say it? At times of public excitement.'

'Quite.'

'Fortunately it was summer time and my grandmother swam to the further bank. The very next week the Bolsheviks came into power and threw into the river many members of the Social-Democratic party.'

'And when the Independence was declared I suppose they threw the Bolsheviks in?'

'By that time,' Count Scherbatcheff said, 'it was winter. Holes had to be cut in the ice.'

That was how the time passed as far as Copenhagen. They arrived there at night and the two Danish young men disembarked. The German commercial traveller remained on board but he never spoke again. He sat alone in the smoke saloon and read the back numbers of *Die Freundschaft* which he had taken the precaution to bring with him. Lushington and Count Scherbacheff walked up from the docks into the town and dined there and went to a cinema. When they arrived back on board they found that there were some more passengers. There was a pile of luggage, but its owners had retired to bed.

4

THEY sailed from Copenhagen early the next morning. Among the new arrivals was another Count. Lushington found this additional Count in the bar. He was a fat man who smelt of brilliantine and sandalwood boxes and his profession was to sell face cream. He made no secret of this and at once showed Lushington a sample of the face cream that he sold. As a slight return Lushington stood him a drink. It was at this juncture that the new Count introduced himself by handing across a card on which were printed the words *Le Comte Michel Bobel* under a coronet. Count Bobel also wore a coronet embroidered on the outside of his shirt immediately over his heart and above it the letter B. It was embroidered in mauve silk and as he did not wear a waistcoat it was possible to see it when he opened his coat and rested his hands on his upper ribs, which he did when emphasising conversational points. He talked French some of the time and said that he was Russian. What race he actually belonged to it was impossible to say. In face he was German, with thick lips and a roll of fat at the back of his neck, but although he talked German he seemed to prefer using French or English and he had evidently an oriental strain, Levantine perhaps or Armenian, that through the working of some Mendelian law had given him more of its colour than his more immediate presumed racial infusions. Lushington said that he himself would not buy any face cream at the moment. Count Bobel said:

'You have seen the ladies, yes?'

'On this boat?'

'Indeed.'

'I have not seen them yet.'

Count Bobel puffed out his cheeks. He was smoking an amber cigarette which he never removed from his lips, so that the smoke from it curled into the eyes of anyone who was standing beside him, making them smart and water. Lushington edged away.

'You like girls?' Count Bobel said. 'The younger one is magnificent. *Exquise.* They came on board at Copenhagen at the same time as myself. They have a great amount of luggage. But even before I had seen that, I could tell that they were ladies of rank. It will be a good voyage.'

Lushington said that he hoped so. He himself was by no means confident after what Count Scherbatcheff had said and, besides, the wind seemed to be getting up. He tried to decide whether or not he would eat any lunch. He had been trying to decide that all the morning. While he was speculating on this point someone outside began to ring a bell. Making up his mind on the spur of the moment at least to see what the meal was going to be, he said:

'That is for luncheon. Shall we go below?'

'*En avant, mon cher.*'

In the dining-saloon the ladies of whom Count Bobel had spoken were sitting at the Captain's table. Lushington habitually sat at the Captain's table and also Count Scherbatcheff, but the German commercial traveller and the two Danish young men had not sat there and the German now sat by himself. Count Scherbatcheff was late for lunch and accordingly had his seat appropriated by Count Bobel, who parried the efforts of the stewardess to eject him. The Captain, a gloomy Swede, watched the tussle but offered help to neither party, and when Count Scherbatcheff arrived he had to sit at the same table as the German. But he sat at the far end of it, away from the German himself, so that he could join in the conversation at the Captain's table.

Lushington looked at the two ladies. One of them was elderly and fidgeted and moped, full of aristocratic worries. The other was much younger, a tall blonde with blue eyes and high cheek-bones, dressed in light-coloured clothes and looking like the leading lady in a German musical comedy. They were talking German to each other, but it was evident that the younger woman had Slav blood. She was not what technically is called beautiful. Her features were not proportioned with enough restraint for that and she was too tall and thin. But she carried with her a certain gorgeousness which was like something that Lucy, too, possessed, and for a moment he was reminded of Lucy, although this woman was not like her in appearance nor in manner. Count Bobel, who was still talking English, French, and German indiscriminately, said:

'And so you have been to Copenhagen, ladies? What a pleasant town in which to spend a holiday. I myself envy you.'

They nodded, the elder one examining Count Bobel with apprehension. The younger one turned and looked at him too and in profile her cheek-bones and long, blacked eye-lashes made an angular pattern against the varnished walls of the dining-saloon. Count Bobel, when he saw that she was looking at him, made his beautiful smile and, eyeing her wedding ring, said:

'And did you in Copenhagen buy many presents for your dear parents, mademoiselle?'

She laughed and shook her head, glancing across the table for a moment to where Lushington was sitting. Her eye-brows were plucked and arched so as to give her an expression of exaggerated indifference to things, but her eyes showed that at some time in the past she had been hurt and made to suffer. Count Bobel said:

'Copenhagen is a very gay city, mademoiselle. I hope that you got into no mischief?'

The Swedish Captain, awakened by the thought of mischief at Copenhagen from the kind of trance into which he was accustomed to fall at meals, said:

'Every year at the same season Frau Mavrin makes this journey. For three years I have taken her back on my vessel. Is not that so, Frau Mavrin? And Baroness Puckler too?'

They said that it was true. They said that they went to Copenhagen to buy their Christmas presents. Neither of them seemed to care much for Count Bobel. Count Bobel himself, however, was quite satisfied with the impression he had made and asked for a second helping of stew and sauerkraut, saying:

'A thousand apologies, madame, that I should have addressed you as mademoiselle, but it seemed impossible to me that one so young should be already married.'

Count Scherbatcheff when he arrived used different methods. He was handicapped from the start by being very angry at having his seat taken away from him, but after this initial setback he settled down into his stride, which was to be very attractive and feline and to talk English. He tried Russian at first, but this was not well received by the ladies. The old lady, Baroness Puckler, was less chilly with Count Scherbatcheff than she had been with Count Bobel, and after a short conversation it turned out that she knew several of his relations although she did not remember the grandmother whom he was on his way to see. But Baroness Puckler made it clear from her manner that in her native town no Russians were to be on her visiting list however friendly she might choose to be on board ship.

Frau Mavrin treated Count Scherbatcheff as she had treated Count Bobel, eyeing him and laughing at his jokes, but not troubling to hide that she took no interest in him at all. Baroness Puckler said to Lushington:

'Does it happen that you know Mr. Da Costa at your legation?'

'I know him very well.'

'He often comes to my house. Ortrud, you have met him too, I think?'

'Indeed he is charming and has such a yellow face.'

'Yes,' said Lushington. 'He has.'

He wondered if Frau Mavrin too was in love with Da Costa. At least it appeared that she had only met him once. He tried to estimate the relationship between these two women. Baroness Puckler behaved like someone who had in her possession a valuable pet, a rare animal that must be looked after constantly in case it should get into mischief or fall into a decline from inattention. But Frau Mavrin, as it were, produced and did showman for Baroness Puckler and yet it was evident that it was really Frau Mavrin herself who was being exhibited and by her very attentions evading any sentimental restraint.

By the end of the meal everyone was great friends with everyone else. The Captain and the German commercial traveller went away and Frau Mavrin, Baroness Puckler, Lushington and the two Counts remained drinking coffee while the two hard-faced stewardesses cleared the table. The boat had begun to roll gently. Frau Mavrin said:

'Sophia, you must tell our fortunes. That will entertain all of us and pass the time.'

'But, my dear Ortrud, do these gentlemen wish that their fortunes should be told? And, besides, the motion of the boat is beginning to make my head ache. Do not you notice it yourself?'

'You must beg her, all of you,' Frau Mavrin said. 'You must press her to tell your fortunes. If you do not do this she will think that you do not wish for your fortunes to be told.'

She looked at Lushington under her heavy lashes and he became aware of contact with her. She dropped her eyes suddenly, like pulling down a blind with a snap. For a moment he felt almost as if he had touched her. Then it was over and he and the Counts were telling the Baroness how much they would enjoy a prognosis. They took some time to persuade her, but at last she said:

'I will fetch my cards and tell the fate of each of you. It will rest on your heads if I foretell evil things.'

She got up and went to her cabin. Count Bobel moved round to the seat next to Frau Mavrin.

'Like this it will be more convenient,' he said.

The sea had become noticeably rougher and some of the beams in the dining-saloon began to creak. Once the coffee cups slid almost off the table and the smell of cocoanut oil seemed to have become more noticeable. There was also an increasingly evil scent of fish. Baroness Puckler returned with a pack of cards. She said:

'They are greasy, but always I use them. Those with the second sight often have a special pack that they prefer to use and such are these.'

Count Scherbatcheff said: 'I fear, Baroness, that you will find my fortune a sad one. The fortune of a man who has lost in the gamble for life. A man who in that game has often thrown the zero.'

Baroness Puckler handed the cards to Lushington to shuffle and cut. Count Bobel lit another cigarette and said:

'I am the King of Hearts. That is my representative card. It bespeaks my character. You agree, all of you?'

Lushington made the cards and cut. Baroness Puckler began to lay them out on the table. Frau Mavrin said:

'And are you going to believe what Sophia tells you?'

'I don't know yet.'

'She has the true gift. She never makes a mistake in her predictions. She will indeed tell you the future.'

'How dangerous.'

'Do you think so?'

Baroness Puckler began counting the cards, checking up their relation to each other. She said to Lushington:

'First I will say what stands round you. Like all your countrymen you are a prey to melancholy. The spleen of Hamlet. I see you in a big building. It is a church or a palace. You hurry through it writing in a book. Many people are round you, men and women, and they too write in books. A great noble who has many enemies rules over you all. And now I see you next to a fair woman. But she belongs to someone else. Quite soon there is a journey across water. The fair woman comes in again. I see her standing next to you. You go among a number of people. All of them are talking scandal. The fair woman goes out of your life. No, no. I see her with you again. Perhaps there are two fair women. You will meet a dark man who is displeased about something. Will you cut again? There are troubles and disturbances. Perhaps even death. You will receive a letter from across water. You will have a disappointment. There is a love affair. Perhaps it is one of the fair women. You will make some money. Not much money. A little money. It arrives in a letter. A small sum, but you will be glad of it. Perhaps it is the great noble who sends it to you. Cut again and wish. You have wished?'

'Yes.'

Baroness Puckler looked at the card.

'You will have your wish. It will be granted to you.'

Frau Mavrin said: 'I see from your fortune that you are a dangerous man. I am curious to know what you wished.'

24

'Are you? But if I tell you I shall not get my wish.'

'It is something wicked I feel sure.'

'Perhaps.'

Count Scherbatcheff was next. He cut the ace of spades and before Baroness Puckler could speak he said:

'Ah, yes. I see. You need not explain it. The card of death. My poor grandmother. I knew that it must come sooner or later. But I feel an affection for her. In spite of her obstinacy I am attached to her.'

The rolling of the ship was becoming more and more apparent and with it strange odours floating up from the galley. Some of the cards fell on to the floor and in picking them up Count Scherbatcheff knocked his head on the edge of the table. The rest of them were full of sympathy for him, but the rolling continued and occupied their attention. Baroness Puckler lifted her hands to her forehead. Lushington held on to the table to steady himself. Count Bobel took out a pocket comb and began to smoothe his hair. Count Scherbatcheff was too dignified to rub his head, but he patted his chest and said:

'I have learned sufficient, my dear Baroness. My poor grandmother. However much I may expect her death it will always be a blow to me when it comes. And now I shall go and lie down for a short time in my cabin.'

He went away suddenly, unexpectedly. He was gone like a flash. They heard a door slam as he arrived below. Count Bobel said:

'It will interest all of you to hear what my fortune will be. I am a person who has had innumerable adventures of all kinds. I am a man of the world. I am interested in everything and naturally a man of that kind is the best subject for the seer. Be sure that you all attend.'

But Baroness Puckler was standing up. She still held her hands to her head. The boat beneath them continued to ride uneasily the swell of the sea. The beams creaked all the time, Baroness Puckler said:

'Another time, Count, another time. Just now like Count Scherbatcheff I go to lie down for a little. Ortrud, I shall see you later.'

Lushington and Count Bobel stood up. Count Bobel said:

'I trust, dear lady, that you are not unwell?'

'It is nothing. Nothing. But I go to lie down.'

Baroness Puckler refused Count Bobel's arm and went away down the stairs that led to the cabins. Lushington, Count Bobel, and Frau Mavrin were left sitting round the table. Lushington himself was becoming aware of a feeling of vertigo, but he was unwilling to leave the field to Count Bobel, although the Count's presence prevented him from making any headway with Frau Mavrin. She sat in her place, assured of herself, almost lovely, making conversation to them both, sometimes staring from under her long eyelashes. The boat heaved about recklessly. The sensation of vertigo was becoming increasingly apparent. Count Bobel, who had left a pile of cigarette ends in the ash-tray, where they burned on incessantly like a small bonfire, said:

'You do not mind, madame, if I smoke a cigar?'

'Not at all.'

'And you, sir?'

'Naturally not.'

'You will smoke one with me. They are good, these. They are a special brand. They come from Batavia and are hard to obtain.'

'Thank you, no,' said Lushington. 'As it happens I think I, too, shall go to my cabin for a little while. I have reached an important point in a book I am reading. It is a detective story and very exciting.'

5

THE sea continued to be choppy. The German commercial traveller lay on his face on the leather seat which ran round the smoke saloon, with his cheek pressed against several copies of *Die Freundschaft*. His expression showed that philosophically he had reached the sphere of complete submission to fate. Lushington in his cabin thought about Frau Mavrin. He also thought about Lucy and remembered that she had said that he must find someone else. Later he felt better and ate a little dinner. Count Scherbatcheff appeared again too and said, rather insincerely, that his stomach was in any case so unsettled that it was unaffected by the motion of the waves. He did not accept, however, the amber cigarette that Count Bobel offered him. Count Bobel therefore smoked it himself and many more after it. He was also heard to ask for cointreau in the bar. The smell of cocoanut oil persisted, especially below deck, but that of fish was kept under better control and towards evening abated considerably.

6

THE wind had dropped a little and Count Scherbatcheff said that the worst was past and it would not be rough for the rest of the voyage. The passengers on board now formed a world of their own and it was difficult to imagine any time when acquaintance had not been limited to this half a dozen and all life proportioned to the boundaries set by the sea.

Lushington sat with the two Counts in the smoke saloon. They were comparing experiences and after a lull in the conversation he said:

'I suppose we are due to arrive tomorrow?'

Count Scherbatcheff, who was unwilling to break the thread of the discussion, said:

'After that you never feel the same towards a woman. It happened to me once with a girl of mine in Munich. I never felt the same to her after that. Never. Our relationship was altered. All was spoilt.'

Count Bobel said: 'You should have taken more care, Count Scherbatcheff. With women you can never be certain. Now in London, Mr. Lushington, how is it with girls? Always I collect addresses. Is it true there are no *maisons*? No *quartier reservé*?'

'Absolutely.'

'That I cannot understand. *Comment s'amuse la jeunesse?*'

'This girl I was speaking of in Munich,' said Count Scherbatcheff, who disliked interruption, 'she was a

Bavarian girl. An art student. I was passionately fond of her.'

Count Bobel said: 'That is like we Russians. It is always the same. We cast our hearts at the feet of women. It is in our nature to give. We do not know restraint. You western peoples little comprehend our ways.'

'She was beautiful,' Count Scherbatcheff said. 'A girl of good family. A girl whom it would be impossible to forget.'

Count Bobel said: 'I too have lived and loved in Munich, Count Scherbatcheff. Who can forget those summer evenings in the gardens of Nymphenburg? Or sunset through the trees at Schleissheim? Not I for one. Though it was long ago. I was connected with a pedicure establishment in that city for several months. A certain girl especially I remember who was employed by the same firm.'

Count Scherbatcheff said: 'It is indeed remarkable that you should mention Nymphenburg. It was in those very gardens that I was accustomed to meet the girl I was telling you of.'

'She was fair,' Count Bobel said, 'and——'

'This girl was dark——'

'Allow me one moment, Count Scherbatcheff——'

'Please, please——'

'And now,' Lushington said, 'I shall walk a little outside before I go to bed. It is an English custom and, besides, my digestion requires that I take some exercise. Good-night. Good-night.'

It was cold on deck. Lushington went to his cabin and put on an overcoat. Then he walked to the forepart of the boat and, leaning over the side, looked at the sea, wintry like that on which the schooner *Hesperus* had sailed. He was feeling a great deal better now. The sea was calm and the hard clearness of the night limited the illusion of space and accentuated the claustrophobia of sea-travel. The ship seemed shut in closely by the waves and the bright wastes of stars. The breeze came faintly across the water as he walked along. He did not at once notice Frau Mavrin, who was standing away from the sea, leaning a little against one of the nondescript subsidiary structures that overspread the deck. When he became aware of her he saw that she was watching him. As he looked she came across the deck towards him and said:

'Do talk to me. I came here for a little before bedtime. It is such a lovely night.'

'The sea is very calm tonight certainly.'

'Where have you been? I have not seen you since dinner. Have you been avoiding me?'

'Avoiding you, Frau Mavrin?'

'No, no. It was silly of me to say that. I did not mean that exactly. And please do not call me Frau Mavrin.'

'I do not know your other name.'

'Ortrud.'

'It suits you. It is a lovely name.'

'Do you think so? Where have you been? Talking to the two Counts?'

'I was sitting smoking with them. That is why I did not see you after dinner.'

'Those two terrible men.'

'Don't you like them?'

Standing beside him she touched his arm.

'You are the only person on board to whom I can talk. That fearful Count Bobel, whom I feel sure is not a count at all. And even Count Scherbatcheff, many of whose cousins I have met. Both of them made extraordinary suggestions to me as soon as I was left alone with them. But I suppose I should not tell you all this.'

'Suggestions?'

'I am a woman of the world. I know men a little. But is

that any reason why they should behave in that way to me?'

'But of course not.'

'With you,' she said, 'I feel safe.'

Not knowing exactly why he did it, Lushington put his arm around her.

'With me,' he said, hoping it would not mean fighting a duel with either of the other two, 'you are safe.'

Later they leaned together arm-in-arm over the side of the boat, watching the sea. Lushington said:

'You are not Russian, are you?'

'Why do you ask?'

'You look a little like a Russian.'

'I am Austrian. You wonder why I am going on this voyage. I will tell you. My family had a small property in Galicia, but we lost all our land at the end of the War. My father would not change his nationality. He had been an officer in the *K. und K.* cavalry. You understand? He did not recognise the partition of the Empire.'

'Exactly.'

'So we went to Vienna and my parents kept a *pension*. I taught dancing. But my father was a man of naturally gay disposition. He rose above his misfortunes and used to lose all the money we earned by the *pension* and the dancing lessons when he played cards. Then my mother, who was a Pole, became despondent and ran away with a Rumanian financier. It is because I look like my mother that you thought I was a Slav.'

'And then what happened?'

'For a time my father and I lived on the bets he won at the local café. No one came to my dancing class. And then one day a foreign professor arranged to have six lessons. Before he had completed the course I was married to him.'

'Did you teach him to dance after you were married?'

'Never.'

'Why not?'

'After we were married he said that there was no more need for him to know how to dance. He only wished to learn in order to find a wife.'

Again she reminded him of Lucy, but because she was different and not because their careers had been a little the same. There was the rather sparkling hardness that gave meaning to what both said, but the force behind it here was all instinctive and unsupported by any of Lucy's semiphilosophic buttresses.

'He is a difficult man,' she said, meaning her husband.

'Older than you?'

'Oh, yes. He is difficult, you know.'

'Does he treat you badly, then?'

'He does not always understand.'

They leaned there together, looking out towards the sea.

'I was so surprised when you kissed me,' she said.

'Were you?'

'I did not know that Englishmen did that sort of thing.'

'Now you know.'

'Now I know.'

They moved from the sea, more conveniently, to a seat beside the wireless cabin. She seemed to him absurdly slim and yielding beneath her heavy coat. At the same time the deck was not in the circumstances an ideal place. She sat there for a time in his arms. Then she said:

'Which of the two Counts shares your cabin?'

'Neither of them. I have a cabin to myself. On the port side.'

'Which side is that? I don't know what that means.'

'There. That side.'

'They say that the sea rolls less on that side. That is the best side to have a cabin.'

'Which side is yours?'

'It is on the other side. At the far end of the passage. But do you find that it rolls much on your side?'

'Not so much as you might think. I am lucky to have a cabin to myself. Don't you agree?'

'Does it roll there more than it is rolling now? What do you think?'

'I don't know. I think it does.'

'It rolls very badly on the side I am on too.'

'You share a cabin with your friend, of course?'

'Yes.'

They did not speak for some minutes. The wind was increasing and had begun to blow shrilly through the rigging, which creaked and strained insistently. The lights were still on in the smoke saloon. The two Counts would talk for some time yet. He said:

'Would you like to come down to my cabin and see if the boat rolls as much on that side as the side that you are on?'

'Yes,' she said. 'It would interest me to see.'

7

IN the cabin, when she gave herself to him, she lost some of her remoteness. This remoteness was a weapon, a protection that she might at any moment reassume. But she put it aside for the time when she gave herself to him. He was surprised and rather shaken, feeling that he had been carried unexpectedly off his feet. Afterwards he watched her. Like Lucy she was thin, but she had not Lucy's effortless, quite amateur loveliness. She was like a very spruce animal. Her skin was not so white as Lucy's. It was tawny, almost olive, and her hair was not so fair. Resting her arm on his shoulder, she said:

'We must meet again. It is a small place and we shall meet again. I am sure that it will be soon.'

'Yes, soon.'

He kissed her.

'You are in love with someone else already, yes?'

'Why should I be?'

'It came in the cards.'

'So it did.'

'Is it true?'

'No.'

'Yes it is. I know. I always know such things.'

'Why do you ask, then?'

'You are in love with someone else and you do this? Are you not ashamed?'

'Anyway, I'm not married, as it appears you are.'

'She is an English girl and she does not love you. I know it is that.'

'How do you know?'

'I am sure of it.'

'Why should you be interested in it at all?'

'You will see. We will meet again and you will tell me all the story. What do you say to that?'

'We shall see.'

'Now I must go.'

'Don't forget this.'

She laughed.

'How absurd. I nearly left it here. Give it to me.'

She turned and slapped his face lightly. Then she opened the door, listened, and went out into the passage. Her perfume, heavy and disturbing, still hung about the cabin. When she had gone Lushington opened the port-hole for a few seconds, but it was so cold that he shut it almost at once. It was rough that night and he could not sleep. He continually thought of Lucy. But he did not think anything definite about her. He merely thought of her.

8

IN the afternoon the air was still clear and they could see a town between the gaps in the islands. The lower part of the town was obscure, hidden in light mists, but there were shapes behind that took on an architectural form. This was their destination. The end of the voyage. Soon they would be set at liberty from the sea. Count Scherbatcheff, who for his health's sake had eaten no lunch, said:

'In the first place let me assure you, Lushington, that the man is not a Russian. It is no doubt equally absurd to suppose that he is a count. His behaviour! Have you noticed it? The way he sits at table. His attitude towards the ladies and especially Frau Mavrin. What could be more repellent? And then the heraldic chinoiserie embroidered all over the front of his shirt. I feel certain that he is a man to be avoided. I take this opportunity of warning you to beware of him. There are a great deal too many men of his type about Europe at the present day passing themselves off as Russians.'

He looked at Lushington through very pale blue eyes. To disembark he was wearing the *béret* with the enamel buttons on it and a raglan overcoat that hung in folds like a cloak. He shook his head and began to walk up and down the deck, sometimes stopping to stamp his feet or beat his arms across his chest.

The ship sailed on, seeming to approach no nearer the town. The hard-faced stewardesses only shrugged their shoulders when asked what time the voyage was coming to an end. Two hours? Three hours? They could not say. It was later that afternoon in the bar, when the view of the town had been hidden unexpectedly by a muddy haze, that Count Bobel said:

'Count Scherbatcheff is a good fellow, Mr. Lushington. He comes of an excellent family. But he is from Little Russia and, like all who come from Little Russia, he has very marked peculiarities. Besides, you must know that his mother was a Georgian princess. He has moreover learned nothing from our country's misfortunes. We of the Russian nobility must face a new order. Times have changed. We are no longer the boyars of John the Terrible. We must curb our pride. Count Scherbatcheff has not yet learned that. He may have a bitter lesson one of these days. Nevertheless he is a sportsman. *Un bon garçon.*'

'What part of Russia do you come from?'

Count Bobel's eyes narrowed a little. His cigarette hung almost vertically from his upper lip and the smoke from it curled gently into Lushington's right eye. The scent of amber hung all round him in a protective cloud. He said:

'My family had several large estates. But they were in a distant part of the country. At a great way off. As you must know, Russia is a very immense country. For a foreigner it is difficult even to imagine the extent of it. And now as we shall be landing in a short time I must inspect again my baggage as it contains commodities about which there may be question at the *douane*. You understand me?'

Lushington went on deck again. Ortrud and Baroness Puckler were there wearing all their coats and scarves and standing beside a cairn of suitcases. The Baroness said:

'Always this affair of getting past the customs and the passport officers. But last time we were lucky and it was

37

all over in less than an hour and a half. Let us hope we shall repeat our good fortune on this occasion.'

Ortrud said: 'It is good that we have reached here before the ice. Often at this time it is frozen up. We have had a lucky voyage.'

Only her eyes, blue and lozenge-shaped, appeared above the collar of her persian-lamb coat. Lushington slipped his arm behind one of the suitcases and touched her hand. She caught one of the fingers between two of hers and said:

'We must all meet again when we have recovered from the stress of the voyage, Mr. Lushington. You will come and have dinner with me and with my husband?'

As they went on towards the shore the islands receded from the town and remained to the right and left in the mist among which they had first appeared. The place came into sight suddenly, huddled up, with blue-green spires and a red and gold cathedral. A castle or palace in grey stone was built on a rampart in a part of the town that was on a higher level than the rest of the houses. The boat passed a fort jutting out into the sea and then entered twisting waterways between wharfs. Here there was accommodation for a navy, but the docks were deserted. Sometimes decrepit tramps rode at anchor, flying a German or Scandinavian ensign, with frozen washing hanging out to dry attached to the lower rigging. There were streets and houses among the docks and looking between these it seemed that ships were moored in the thoroughfares of the town itself, so that quite suddenly Lushington thought again of Lucy, vividly, as if she were standing beside him as they moved forward. These ships among the buildings recalled her to him, bringing back a day they had spent together in the country when, coming through some trees towards the sea, funnels and masts appeared before them a few fields away, rising out of hedges and ploughland, jagged and coloured gaudily against

38

the green, damp English morning. These unlikely hulls by some configuration of an estuary had seemed cut off and permanently land-locked, part of the strangeness of the countryside. Liners built up among the hedges. The day had been doubly notable for Lucy's release from the higher pessimism and the ships here now reminded him of her as she had come through the trees with him and stopped all at once, her hair blowing across her face as they stood and looked at the painted funnels.

But that had been months before, he thought. This was another country. Something altogether different.

The ship had ceased to make headway and a motor-boat put out from one of the quays and puffed towards them. An officer wearing a sword came on board and a weary civilian with a shaved head and an eyeglass. This last person carried a heavy instrument as for jacking up a lorry. With this contrivance, which proved to be a survival from the early days of printing, he stamped all the passports which he considered to be in order and at the same time was persuaded by Count Bobel to accept a cigar. At last they landed and Lushington drove to the hotel, where he found a note from Da Costa, who apologised for having been unable to meet the boat. Lushington had dinner and went to bed early. He was tired after the journey.

9

THE hotel was unexpectedly large, with palm trees in pots placed at intervals round the lounge. There were two doors at the entrance, one of them so heavy that only very strong people could get into the hotel at all without help and even those who managed to push it open, unassisted by the hall porter, were often swept back into the street at the very moment when they had seemed on the point of gaining admittance. From the middle of the morning onwards business men sat in the wicker chairs of the lounge and drank coffee or *schnapps* and worked out sums for each other in pencil on the backs of envelopes. Flosshilde, the reception clerk, sat at her desk all day long watching the business men. She had red hair and was fat for her age and she wore an engagement ring made of large imitation diamonds. She spoke a dozen words of all languages and usually she had the lounge well under control. Sometimes, but not often, when the business men were very tiresome, she lost her head and the manager had to be sent for. Now she stood over Lushington while he filled up forms for the police dossier of foreigners.

'See!' she said. 'You have not written. The profession of mother's father?'

'I don't know it.'

'*So?*'

'No.'

'Write *private*, then. And the date of marriage of father and mother?'

'I can't remember.'

'They are truly married?'

'They always say so.'

This was a critical situation. Flosshilde thought. She said:

'Write any time before your birthday. But write it a year before.'

'All right. But give me another pen.'

Opposite the hotel was the National Theatre, in stucco, Palladian and undistinguished. In the Russian time it had been the Opera House. Near-by was the Bourse. All this was in the Low Town, where most of the buildings were modern and the streets were broad. In the High Town on the other side of the river there were medieval houses made of wood and the streets were narrow and broken by steps and archways. The place was quite unreal, Lushington noticed. Flosshilde said that there would be snow soon. When that came this unreality would be absolute, although as a set-piece the scene would remain unstylised. Because the unreality was something in itself. Not the product of historical association nor even the superimposed up-to-dateness. It was related perceptibly to the foreground of sea. The weather was not unpleasantly cold and the air was astonishingly clear. But there would be snow soon, Flosshilde said, because it was already late in the month.

IO

DA COSTA'S flat was in the High Town. There was a shiny white-painted stove in the sitting-room, built out into the middle of the floor, and a bookcase with all Da Costa's books in it, piled up anyhow, some of them facing the wrong way. It was a large, uncomfortable room, greatly overheated, the sort of room that Da Costa was accustomed to inhabit. Lushington sat there looking through the double windows at the Baltic. Da Costa, a dark young man with a greenish, horse-shaped face, stood beside him, also watching the sea, his mouth a little open as if at any moment he were going to laugh. The two surfaces of glass were faulty in the middle, so that the spires of the Lutheran churches seemed to have broken away from their swollen bases as they narrowed up. The spires of the Lutheran churches were green and the Russian cathedral was built of red brick with five gold cupolas. The flat was high up and the sea was a long way off beyond the docks, but to the right and left of the town it was possible to distinguish where buildings ended suddenly in stretches of sand and pines. On the other side of the house the bedroom looked down on to a square in which a few market stalls were set up once a week, and opposite these was the new railway station, designed on a substratum of *modernismus,* with pylons and tumid, angular caryatids. This was in red stone, the same red as the Russian cathedral, and it stood out uncompromisingly against the sky, which was steel-coloured and opaque. Da Costa said:

'Sometimes, as an Englishman, I feel a little inferior about my name in a country where so many people are descended from seventeenth-century adventurers and are called everyday names like Baron Morgan or Count Mackintosh. Or even, like the Chilean consul, merely Smith.'

Lushington laughed. He was experiencing the feeling of irritation brought on by seeing again an old friend from whom he had been separated for many months. Da Costa, he noticed, felt the same, and Lushington knew that Da Costa was wondering when he himself would begin to talk about Lucy. It was a point upon which he had not yet made up his mind. He was thinking at that moment of his own satisfaction that Da Costa should care so little about her and at the same time of his annoyance that Da Costa should care so little while he himself cared a good deal. But he knew by experience that if his own affection for Lucy ever seemed to show signs of diminishing Da Costa was accustomed to show uneasiness because this seemed to lessen the value of Lucy's feelings for himself. On that account at least Lushington decided to say nothing of Ortrud. Besides, the thought of her disturbed him and made him feel curiously more amiable towards Da Costa.

Pope was in the room too, moving secretively as if he were tidying up, sometimes pausing to examine letters or papers that Da Costa had left lying about or making scraps of introvert conversation. Pope had an unhealthy complexion, strangely discoloured, mineral rather than flesh, and hair so fair that it was nearly white. He hurried about the room, touching everything. He spoke always gently as if he were talking to a sick person. Gently but with insistence. Da Costa leaned so close to the window that his nose touched it and made a steamy mark on the near pane.

At this he retreated his face a little and turned towards the east, where on the high ground beyond the industrial quarter were low, green-painted buildings like dolls' houses, government offices in the Russian time, now made into tenements. Lushington watched the people passing below the window. The streets were crowded at this time of day, mostly with men in black overcoats and astrakhan caps and goloshes. There were also staff officers who carried under their arm black portfolios, and a few boy and girl students in coloured peaked caps on their way home from the University.

The evening light came into the room with curious slowness, brightening and emphasising the colour schemes of mauve and Venetian red which the late owner, one of the Rumanian secretaries, had instituted and which Pope would not allow Da Costa to alter. Pope began arranging in order of precedence all the invitation cards on the mantelpiece. When he was satisfied with their sequence he addressed himself to Da Costa. He said:

'It always interests me to do this, sir. Social life has always had a great attraction for me and I for it. It comes out in my ways. I notice it myself when I am dealing with others. It is something in myself. I have no control over it. By that I mean that I do not try to prevent myself from exercising this quality, because I see that it is a desirable thing that when such feelings exist they should be encouraged. My family have often commented on the difference between me and them. For example they always call me the Duke.'

Da Costa laughed. He did not answer or turn round. The mark of steam on the inner window became wider than before. Lushington shuffled with his feet. Pope began to smile quietly to himself and set about brushing the crumbs from the table with a rolled-up copy of *The*

Gazette. Then he patted a cushion and moved it from the place where it had been thrown.

'You see, my family think a great deal of me,' he said. 'I often tell them that they flatter me too much.'

Outside, the fading evening, giving no warning, had become night. The dark steeples could still be seen among the dim lights. Pope went towards the window and began to draw the blinds. He said:

'I took the liberty of borrowing Freud's *Psychopathology of Life* from your bookcase, sir. It is my free night tomorrow and should like to spend it reading. I often read lying on my bed. I hope you have no objection, sir.'

Da Costa came to with a jerk. He said:

'No, no. Read it anywhere you like. And in any position.'

'Is there anything more this evening, sir?'

'No, that's all.'

'Good-night, sir. Good-night, sir.'

'Good-night, Pope.'

'Good-night.'

Pope went away. Da Costa said:

'That was Pope. I've arranged for him to valet you. He doesn't have much to do and he said he'd like to take the job on. I inherited him from the last man who was here. He's a curious fellow, as you see. Rather a character.'

'But I don't like characters.'

'I know you don't. Neither do I. But we can't always have what we like. You had better take Pope on. I should perhaps warn you that he is sometimes rather inquisitive. Still, he is a good valet.'

'I can't possibly afford a valet.'

'You need not pay him much. You must have someone to look after your clothes. The hotel servants won't touch them. Anyway, I've arranged it with Pope and he is going to call you tomorrow. He's a man with a lot of personality.'

'Why didn't you tell me all this when he was here?'

Da Costa laughed again, but without reference to any particular matter. He changed his weight from his right foot to his left and began to whistle through his teeth. Lushington said:

'And how are the Communists?'

'Splendid. They blew up the new gas-works the other day. At least that is supposed. Either they or the works manager, who was, it appears, a very erratic man. As everything is blown up it is hard to say. It is a pity, because architecturally they were of considerable beauty.'

'Do you ever come in contact with the Soviet legation?'

'Not as a rule. But you ought to. I met one of their secretaries the other day at a tea-party. We were both lodged in a corner and he thought I was an American engineer on his way out to some mines in Russia and I thought he was a French author on his way back. They have invented an entirely new form of boredom, like the worst moments of being in the boy scouts at one's preparatory school. He was a fine example of it.'

'Do you think I shall be able to get any stuff about communism for the paper?'

'Oh, yes. Plenty of stuff. There might easily be a revolution. There have been several outbreaks in countries next door. But a political assassination is about the best thing you can really rely on. There hasn't been one for some time and everyone is getting heartily sick of everyone else.'

'What's it like, being here?'

'An amusing town. I enjoy it. There is Maxim's and the Café Weber and the Station Restaurant and if you've been to all those you can listen to the wireless. You can pick up all sorts of peculiar places from here.'

He laughed again, deafeningly, as if he were going to go

off his head at any moment. Lushington lit a cigarette. Da Costa said:

'Fortunately you have come out here in time for the annual ball given by the nobility. You will be able to write something about that for your beastly paper.'

'Is it a good show?'

'Yes. Excellent. If you like that sort of thing.'

'Where are we going tonight?'

'To the Café Weber and then Maxim's. Maxim's is the night-club. To tell the truth, I have only been there once myself, and that was the night after I arrived for the first time. Two others are coming to dinner. Curtis Cortney, who is third secretary at the American legation, and a fellow called Waldemar.'

'Tell me about them.'

'Waldemar is a soldier. A captain in one of the two cavalry regiments. The 2nd Uhlans, I think. Or perhaps it is the 1st. He isn't really a captain, but he had an appointment at the Ministry of Defence, cleaning out the ink-pots or something of the sort, and everybody calls him Captain.'

'And Cortney?'

'He is a fine chap too. I believe he's a Southerner, but I can't really remember. Perhaps he isn't. I wish their Minister was, though. I like Southerners.'

'What's he?'

'He's whatever you are when you are not a Southerner. He is not a professional diplomat, of course, so that one should not expect too much. That's their system.'

'What is?'

'They give their best diplomatic posts to business men who need a rest or lawyers who have flown a bit near the wind in their own country. They send publishers to the more important capitals, but the people here have to put up

47

with smaller fry. But you'd be surprised to see how soon most of them pick it up. Still, poor Cortney, who is, of course, in their permanent service, used to go through agonies with the last Minister, who could not tie his white tie. It once came undone during a Presidential reception.'

'By the way, Lucy sent her love,' said Lushington, who was not greatly interested in the administration of the United States' diplomatic service.

'Lucy? Oh, did she? How is she? Why doesn't she come out here for a bit?' said Da Costa.

He laughed again vacantly and, to prevent Lushington going on about Lucy, began to hum. But his presence, slowly getting to work like the warming up of an engine, had begun to condition in Lushington renewed thoughts of Lucy and, although Da Costa was not the person with whom from preference he would have discussed her, he was the only one available, being almost certainly the sole human being in the country who had ever heard her name. Lushington said, above the humming:

'I thought she was looking better when I came away.'

He was considering other remarks to make with which to follow up this one when the door-bell rang. Da Costa said:

'This must be Waldemar. I will let him in.'

He went out into the hall and returned almost at once with a young man in uniform who still had his fur cap on his head. The young man looked nervous. He was clean-shaved and wore pince-nez. His double-breasted military overcoat had a high waist and broad sheepskin collar. He clicked his heels, saluted, and said:

'Waldemar!'

Da Costa said: 'He is introducing himself. This is Captain Waldemar. Captain Waldemar—Mr. Lushington.'

Waldemar said in quite good English:

'Pleased to meet you, Mr. Lushington.'

Da Costa said: 'Take your coat and sword off, Waldemar, and we'll have a drink.'

Waldemar unhooked his sword and propped it up in the corner of the room among Da Costa's shooting-sticks and golf clubs. Underneath his overcoat he wore a khaki tunic, well cut but very tight, and a pair of blood-red riding breeches with a yellow stripe down each leg. He seemed rather bothered and passed his hand once or twice round the inside of his cruelly high collar. Then he sat down and said to Lushington:

'You have been playing rugby in England, yes?'

Da Costa, pulling the cork out of a bottle, said:

'No, no. Of course he hasn't. I've told you about that before, Waldemar. You read too many of the wrong sort of English books.'

Waldemar laughed a little and adjusted his pince-nez, but he seemed relieved. Lushington said to him:

'I hear we are going to Maxim's tonight.'

'You like dancing?' Waldemar said. 'There is dancing there. And there are girls.'

'I expect you go there often?'

'No. Not often. Two years ago I was there. It was Christmas time. It was very jocose.'

Da Costa said: 'It's an amusing place. I remember it well. The girls are very good-looking. They are mostly Russian, I believe. You don't have to dance with them if you don't want to. I expect that bell is Cortney arriving.'

He went out into the hall again and came back this time with an American dressed in the English manner and wearing a small fair moustache, trimmed so that it appeared to be false. Da Costa, who was evidently embarrassed by this new arrival as much as he himself embarrassed Waldemar, took the American by the arm and shouted to the others: 'This is Mr. Curtis Cortney. This is a compatriot of mine, Curtis. You know Captain Waldemar already, I think.'

Lushington shook hands with Cortney, who said with a conversational burr as sweet and low as the *vox humana* of some mighty cinema organ:

'Mr. Lushington, I hope that we shall be great friends.'

Da Costa began laughing again and, standing on one leg, yelled:

'Well, Curtis, what's it to be? A high-ball?'

Lushington said to Waldemar:

'How well you talk English.'

Da Costa said: 'Don't sit there paying each other compliments. Come and help mix these drinks.'

Cortney said: 'So we're going to Maxim's tonight. It's strange that I never seem to go there. Only been there once in all the months I've been here.'

'Lovely girls,' said Waldemar, rather unconvincingly, and there was a pause. Waldemar patted his soft black leather riding-boots that wrinkled round his ankles. Lushington said to Cortney:

'Have you been posted here long?'

'Since last fall.'

'How do you like it?'

Cortney said: 'Mr. Lushington, for two years I was at Buenos Aires. Do you know that I just couldn't stop there. I used to wake up in the morning and tell myself that I couldn't stand for those modern boulevards any longer. I used to say why can't I get away to somewhere where there is some history, some romance. And then I got my transfer. Hell, what a day that was, the day I got my transfer. Why, there wasn't a happier man in all B.A. And now when I run my tub each morning I can look through the window and see those ancient grey walls of stone and I think of the old-time knights—*ritters,* they call them here—who caused them to be raised and my heart beats maybe a trifle faster and sometimes I can almost hear the clash of swords on breastplates, and I tell myself no, no, all that was in the days gone by. Ah, Captain Waldemar, it's a great heritage, this little old land of yours. No wonder you're proud of your independence.'

Waldemar said: 'Yes, yes, Mr. Cortney. You love romance. Like you I too love romance. When I was young also I would think how romantic to go to the Wild West. To fight Indians. Or to be English. To have colonies. Always it was childish dream of mine that I should go out to the English colonies. You understand me? It was not a practical thought. It was schoolboy imagining of mine. The dream of a schoolboy not yet grown up.'

Cortney said: 'Captain Waldemar, that's a great idea of yours, but it's not just what I intended to convey. It's a fine viewpoint for a young man, though it may not be my own, if you understand me.'

Waldemar said: 'Nevertheless the English are an elegant race. A nation of dandies. It was a great surprise to me when I saw English officers carrying walking-sticks. Here we may not carry sticks when we are in uniform. It is forbidden. We may not carry sticks unless we are lame.'

Da Costa said: 'Here, drink this, Waldemar, and don't talk so much.'

Cortney turned to Lushington and said: 'I expect I'm just naturally romantic. But that's how the place gets me. And I'll swear it will get you that way too.'

They dined that evening at the Café Weber in a wide room done up in a modern German style. Da Costa, whose nerves were bad, talked most of the time and laughed at all his own jokes. Waldemar and Cortney were evidently used to him. Both seemed to like him, although Waldemar, regarding him as a typical Englishman and as such prepared for the worst, was a little afraid of him. Waldemar himself was a quiet, studious young man whom circumstances rather than taste seemed to have brought to the high calling of arms. He was shy and his tunic was a great deal too tight, and whenever Da Costa asked him whether or not he would eat a certain dish he always said 'Perhaps' as a polite method of throwing the onus of choosing on Da Costa. This had the combined effect of annoying Da Costa and holding up the progress of the meal. At moments even Cortney would say:

'Now then, Captain, show some military decision.'

Cortney at times seemed unnerved by Da Costa's general appearance and manner, but most of all by his clothes, which, as always, looked as if they had been made by a good tailor for someone of quite different shape. Lushington saw him give sidelong glances at Da Costa's waistcoat, which continually worked up above the top of his trousers. The food and wine in the restaurant were like the decorations, heavy and pretentious. As the meal advanced Waldemar became more confident and told them about himself and his life:

'For a year I was in France. At the military school of St. Cyr. One would have to get up at four o'clock in the morning. There was no breakfast. Only very strong black coffee. Sometimes it was too strong for me to drink. There was an English officer there with me. Always he would say that he could not become accustomed to there being no breakfast. He was called Macgregor. It was always that. Macgregor could not become accustomed to that.'

'Ah,' said Cortney, 'you English. You're a great race, but you have your limitations.'

II

MAXIM'S was a small and undistinguished night-club with
a gallery running round it and, instead of being done-up in
modern German, it had been treated freely in the later
manner of French second-empire style. The band, who
were called *Bristol Mondial Boys,* sat at the end of the
room. Their name was written on the drum and they were
playing *O Katerina* while a few couples danced. Waldemar
said:

'You see they have a telephone on every table. Very
modern, you see?'

Cortney said: 'If anyone calls us up you'll have to answer
them, Captain. I've done all my telephoning for today at
the office.'

At the next table two conscripts in baggy uniforms with
pinched, intellectual faces stood up to attention and one of
them upset his drink. Waldemar inclined his head and
they sat down again. Two girls were at the table on the
other side. One of them was dark and wore the approxima-
tion of a riding-habit, an indeterminate affair in bottle-
green, and the other, a sulky-looking blonde with hair *à la
pompadour,* was in black evening dress. They were drinking coffee and lost no time in indicating that they would
be prepared to accept an invitation to supper.

'Shall we get them over?' said Da Costa, rather threaten-
ingly, in case any of the others might say yes, but everyone
was opposed to the suggestion. Da Costa, who had now
become something of the school bully, a nervous state

engendered by finding himself in a night-club, said:

'Come on, Waldemar, pull yourself together and tell all these waiters that we're not going to drink champagne, but they're to get some brandy at once and mind it has a recognisable label on the bottle.'

They sat down and watched the dancers, a mixed party, Waldemar explained, mostly business men with their wives, except a major in the artillery dancing with his fiancée, who played Ibsen heroine parts at the National Theatre, and a long way off the American Minister, who was giving supper to the leading lady from the touring German production of *Gräfin Maritza*. It was some time before Lushington noticed Count Bobel dancing with an elderly woman, who showed by her demeanour that she was paying for the evening's entertainment. The Count bowed to Lushington as he danced past their table. Da Costa said:

'What curious friends you always seem to have.'

'Not at all. Why should you think so?'

'Who is he?'

'A beauty specialist. A count. I met him on the boat coming over here.'

'A typical acquaintance of yours.'

'Do you think so? In any case I see nothing out of the ordinary in my knowing him. He seemed a very normal sort of person.'

The manager of the place stood near the table, moving round it at intervals to examine Lushington, Da Costa and Cortney at different angles. He was not interested in Waldemar. The girls at the next table were not interested in Waldemar either, as they and the manager were equally familiar with the rates of army pay. The manager had a moustache, side-whiskers and a frock-coat. When he had inspected the table from all sides he came very close and said:

'English?'

Da Costa said: 'Yes. Of course I am English. Why do you ask?'

The manager said: 'Very well. Yes, please.'

Da Costa bowed to show that the conversation was at an end, but the manager lingered by the table. He seemed to have something on his mind. He said:

'I was officer in Russian Army. I was major. I was on General Staff.'

Cortney said: 'Well, Major, you've got a nice little place here.'

'Revolution came. All was gone. Now am here.'

Lushington said: 'Rather a change.'

The manager said: 'You want to meet girls. I can arrange it. Good girls. One speak English.'

'Not at the moment.'

This reply appeared so far-fetched that the manager was for the moment at a loss for words. He therefore retreated and consolidated his position. He said:

'I was on General Staff. I pass examination staff-school and was breveted General Staff.'

Da Costa, whose nerves were showing no sign of abating, said:

'Was it fun being on the General Staff.'

The manager said: 'Often when in a new place you feel lonely. Want company. One girl speak English. I present you. Good girl. *Everyone* say good girl.'

'Not yet.'

The manager seemed perplexed. Someone had made a false move. He showed his teeth again.

'Good girls,' he said, but with lessening conviction.

This conversation might have continued indefinitely, but at that point in its development somebody in the band struck a gong and all the lights went out. A mauve spotlight was switched on to the dancing floor and a fat girl in trousers and a Spanish hat came to the centre of the room and with castanets began to sing:

> '. . . *for I'm one of de nuts from Barcelona,*
> *I pliquety-plonque,*
> *My casa-bionque . . .*'

As she sang she danced round the room snapping her castanets in front of each table. The audience received these representations stoically, with the exception of one of the business men who had had too much to drink and who made faces at her while she was executing these movements for his benefit. After a time the lights went on again and the manager was found to be far away. He was ushering in a new party of clients: two women, a man in a white tie and an officer of some rank with a decoration hanging at his throat. At the next table the two conscripts stood rigid. And then Lushington saw that one of the two women was Ortrud.

She came across the room, moving rather superbly. When she saw them she stopped at the table and held out her hand. As they got up she said:

'I told you we should meet quickly again in so little a city. You remember that I said that?'

'I am glad it has been so soon.'

'I present to you,' she said, 'Major-General of Infantry Kuno and Frau Major-General of Infantry Kuno. And this is Herr Legation-Secretary Diaz.'

The General beamed. He was rather more than five feet high and he wore white kid gloves. His wife was dressed in a tippet. Mr. Diaz had a hooked nose and a blue chin and was the unathletic sort of Latin-American. The General jingled his spurs, clanked his sword a little so that the

56

sword-knot swung backwards and forwards, and bowed. Ortrud said:

'The Herr Major-General of Infantry speaks only our language.'

General Kuno nodded and showed his teeth in friendship at Lushington, who nodded and grinned fiercely in return. Lushington said:

'How is Baroness Puckler?'

'Come and speak to me at my table before you go away from here tonight. I will tell you about her. And besides I should myself like to see you again.'

She put her head a little on one side and smiled. Her party moved on towards their table. The arrival of General Kuno had thrown Waldemar into a great state of nerves. Da Costa said:

'You seem to have more friends here than I have. How did you meet Frau Mavrin?'

'On the boat.'

'Do you make all your friends on boats?'

'Some on trains. But who exactly is she?'

'Who is she? Don't you know who she is? What an extraordinary fellow you are. Her husband is Professor of Psychology at the University here. Didn't she tell you? He's a very clever man. An international reputation, almost.'

'What is she like?'

'What's she like? Well, I imagine you know more about her than I do. You were almost alone with her in an open boat for several days. For all the privacy there is on those boats coming out here one might as well be on a raft.'

Cortney, who had been occupied during the past few minutes in glancing furtively at the American Minister, who with the help of the German leading lady was energetically lowering his country's prestige at the far end of the room, began to listen to the conversation again and said:

'If it's Frau Mavrin that you're talking of, I'll tell you Frau Mavrin is a great little lady. She's got poise, she's got dignity, she's got sense of position. She's a sophisticate who knows the worth of simplicity. She's a girl any country should be proud of. She's Frau Mavrin and we all of us love her for it.'

Da Costa said: 'Your chief was talking about her the other day and said she was a tough baby, whatever that may mean. He said she was the sort of dame who if she'd been taken in adultery would have caught the first stone and thrown it back.'

'I'll say he sometimes seems to lack a proper reverence for women although he is my chief. But he doesn't mean it. It's just his hard-boiled way of expressing himself.'

Da Costa said: 'Well, we all of us have our disillusioned moments. I expect your chief does just like the rest of us. In spite of the fun he seems to be having tonight. Come on, Waldemar. Have some more of this. Don't mope.'

Lushington said: 'She's an Austrian, isn't she?'

'Viennese. I fancy she got rather mixed up in some of the gay life there at some point. *Tales from the Vienna Woods* and so on.'

The band, after playing *O Katerina* faster and faster, had now switched over to *Komm mit nach Varasdin*. The girl in the riding-habit and the one with the hair *à la pompadour* got up and began to dance together. They gravitated to the centre of the room, where, hovering, they attempted a charleston. Once when they passed the table the cross-looking one said 'Hullo, mister,' to Cortney. Da Costa said:

'Of course they don't really like one coming here much at the legation. In fact when the Old Man was here he once warned me against the place. However, Bellamy won't bother even if he hears of it and the new Minister is bound to get rid of me anyway.'

'What will you do if he does?' Lushington said.

'I don't know. I may go and dig in Crete or somewhere like that. I've always wanted to do that.'

Cortney said: 'Fortunately our Service does not enforce such a rigid code of personal behaviour. The American People wouldn't think any the worse of us for coming to a dump like this. In fact they'd think we were crazy if we didn't throw a wild party once in a while. Look at the life we lead. What sort of a week have you got ahead of you? I take it you're going to the d'Almeidas' on Tuesday?'

'And dining with the new Japanese that night.'

'I'm not in on that, but there's the Danish *thé dansant* the day after and dinner at the Castellinis' for the Gomez reception, and they're burying Parapapadoukos on Thursday and I'm going to play bridge with the Zadeks that night.'

'I'm going to all those, so that we shall meet several times. Then I shall see you on Friday night at the Bellamys', I hope, and are you going to the Ninitch lunch at the Café Weber?'

'Naturally, and the Jakobsens' that afternoon.'

'That's fine,' Da Costa said, 'because I must have a word with you in the near future about something Bellamy wants to know with regard to imported textiles. I expect some opportunity will turn up for discussing the matter.'

Lushington, who had not been listening because he was watching Ortrud and her party, said:

'Who is General Kuno?'

Waldemar said: 'For the time he commands the police. He is a very strong man. Some do not like him. During the Civil War he executed many people. But he is not so important now as then. Not so important as some of the colonels. Some of the colonels are very important men.'

Count Bobel, who was seated some way off at a table in the gallery, appeared to be having an uninteresting evening with his partner, who wore a chignon. He continually turned round and smiled at Lushington and pointed below the gallery to indicate where Ortrud was sitting. Lushington smiled back wanly, hoping that others would not see him.

They watched the dancing. Ortrud went round the room once, doing a tango with the South American Diaz, but as she passed her own table she said something to him and they stopped and sat down. The fat girl appeared again several times, variously dressed in man's evening clothes, peasant costume, and as Columbine. There was also a man who did step-dancing and held knives in his mouth. The atmosphere was warm and some ladies were fanning themselves with the paper fans that had been handed round. The manager threw a few coloured streamers, but after a time he became tired of doing this and sat at a table near the band and had some tea.

It was getting late. Waldemar yawned once or twice behind his hand. Da Costa said:

'Is it bedtime, do you think?'

Lushington said: 'Before we go I must speak to Frau Mavrin. I should like to see her again.'

As he said this he saw that Ortrud and her party had paid their bill and were coming across the room. General Kuno clattered across the dance floor and once more the two conscripts stood up. Ortrud came to the table and said:

'Will not you and your friends come to my apartment for a few minutes before you go home? Mr. Da Costa and Mr. Cortney and you, Herr Hauptmann, whom I have not met yet? You will come?'

She smiled at the others. She watched them from under her absurdly arched eyebrows. Waldemar excused himself on the ground of an early parade he had unexpectedly to attend the following morning, but Da Costa and Cortney said that they would like to come. Ortrud said:

'Then it will be only you three and Mr. Legation-Secretary Diaz. The General and Madame have decided to go home.'

Everyone bowed to everyone else and after a slight disturbance about the bill in which Waldemar had to act as interpreter they left the table. As they went the girl with hair *à la pompadour* said: 'Hey, hey, mister, you come with us, isn't it?'

Da Costa said: 'No, madam, it is nothing of the sort,' and they passed on through the bar towards the door.

In the outer room of the premises the tired, hunched-up man sitting on one of the high stools at the bar turned out to be Count Scherbatcheff, who said:

'Good-night, Lushington. I suppose the manager of this place told you that he was a Russian?'

'Yes.'

'I supposed that he would.'

Count Scherbatcheff shook his head gloomily. Lushington said: 'How did you find your grandmother?'

'She was obstinate. She is an old woman and she likes her own way. You are English. In England you do not make scenes. But my grandmother does not try to control herself. She screams. She throws herself on the floor.'

Seeing Ortrud, Count Scherbatcheff jumped off his stool and kissed her hand. Lushington introduced Da Costa and Cortney. Waiters hung round expectantly, hoping that the festivities were going to begin all over again. Cortney said:

'*Enchanté,* Count. A good friend of mine called

Vanoppen married a Princess Alexandrovna Scherbatcheff in Boston the other day. The Princess is a relative of yours, no doubt?'

Count Scherbatcheff said: 'No, no. No relation. I know of whom you speak. Nor is she a princess. My grandmother was complaining about her only this evening.'

He leaned against the bar and patted his chest.

'I still suffer a great deal from the stomach,' he said. They commiserated and left him leaning against the bar.

'Poor man,' said Ortrud. 'But my husband would never allow me to bring a Russian into the house.'

Cortney said: 'Count Scherbatcheff seems a splendid fellow. One of the best. But I guess he made an error about Princess Alexandrovna Scherbatcheff. Why, she came from one of the best families in Russia. Vanoppen wouldn't have made a mistake about a thing like that. I know him too well to think he'd done that. But they're strange, these old-world aristocrats, sometimes in the things they say about each other.'

They managed to get into one drosky. Diaz, who was good-looking but of weak character, was elbowed away from Ortrud by Lushington and Cortney. Lushington held one of her hands under the rug and wondered whether Cortney was holding the other one. Da Costa from choice sat opposite them. Lushington was relieved to find that Ortrud seemed to know neither Da Costa nor Cortney too well. His own relief surprised him and he speculated upon her friendship with Diaz.

12

THE drosky stopped in front of a block of flats in the University quarter. They entered a cramped lift which they worked themselves by pressing a button. At one point it showed signs of stopping between two floors, but it recovered and ascended the rest of the way in short jerks. They reached one of the higher floors at last, where the lift came to rest.

The Mavrins' flat was unnecessarily full of furniture and pictures of all sorts, including an oleograph of the Emperor Franz-Josef and a cuckoo clock. Ortrud turned on the light and said: 'A moment and I will make tea. I know that Englishmen always like tea. Am I not right?'

They sat down. Ortrud fetched some cups and saucers. Diaz tried to help her, but she told him not to interfere and he retired to sit down with the others. They waited. Then the inner door of the room opened and a tall elderly man with a shaggy moustache and wearing a dressing-gown stood on the threshold. Slowly he came into the room. He was clearly surprised to see so many guests at this hour. He said:

'Ach, Ortrud——'

'Speak English, Panteleimon, these gentlemen are English and do not understand our language.'

'Ach, so?'

'Mr. Lushington, this is my husband.'

Professor Mavrin stood there for a few moments collecting himself, rubbing his eyes with one hand and smoothing down his hair with the other. He seemed sleepy. Then he bowed and shook everyone by the hand, and said:

'Gentlemen, I am delighted to see you all.'

Ortrud said: 'Panteleimon, do not you think that your clothes are a little incorrect now that we have friends to see us? A little informal?'

'My dear, I have but now come from bed.'

'But, my dear husband, would it not be right to wear something more in keeping? That is my thought.'

'My dear, you suggest that I put on my clothes again?'

'Mr. Legation-Secretary Diaz has full evening dress. These gentlemen wear the smoking. Should we, their hosts, appear in less?'

'You wish that I put on evening dress again, my dear wife?'

'Would it not be becoming, Panteleimon?'

'Very well, my dear wife. What you think is no doubt best.'

The Professor turned to the others. He said:

'You will excuse me for a few moments, gentlemen. I fear that I have appeared in unsuitable attire. It is my hope that you will perhaps forgive me.'

He drew his dressing-gown around him and went through the door by which he had come in. He looked rather noble in his simple dressing-gown, like a medieval abbot or one of the Burghers of Calais. Ortrud continued to prepare tea. Cortney said:

'Frau Mavrin, what I marvel at in this little country of yours is your home life. Now in America, I hope not too late, we are realising what a sacred institution the home is and how it is threatened by the stress of modern life. It is in the home that the children are being raised that the nation of the future will be proud of, and it's in the home that the finest flower of our womanhood should find its true place. Now that's a lesson it seems to me that this country will never have to learn.'

'Oh, Mr. Cortney, you are so kind.'

'It's just the truth, Frau Mavrin.'

'But then I am really Austrian.'

Cortney made a few passes in the air as if he were conducting an imaginary orchestra of great size and through his teeth he hummed a few bars of the second strain from *The Blue Danube*.

'That's just it, Frau Mavrin,' he said. 'That's just it.'

Diaz, who saw the party developing along lines that no South American could tolerate, made some excuse about never drinking tea and, after spending what seemed to Lushington an age kissing Ortrud's hand, went away. Ortrud said:

'I am not sorry that he has gone. When he first came out here I thought that he was such a nice young man. You understand? He dances well. He is always so attentive. But then I find that I do not like him so much.'

Cortney said: 'Frau Mavrin, you can't be too careful. You must always bear in mind that the attitude of a Latin to a woman is not the one that we Nordic peoples have been brought up to. They do not think along the same lines as we do. They sometimes fail to appreciate that conception of chivalry that is instilled into the Anglo-Saxon from his birth up. Is not that so, Mr. Lushington?'

'Absolutely.'

Da Costa said: 'Come, come, don't forget the hot Portuguese blood that flows in my own veins.'

Ortrud said: 'Ah, I think you are right. I am certainly glad that he has gone. I feel more safe.'

She poured out tea for them and gave them sweet biscuits from a tin box. In this room she looked not at all different from what she had been at Maxim's or on the sea. She was nearly beautiful. Lushington was surprised, because he had expected her to change when he had become accustomed to her appearance and when he had seen her in her own surroundings. He watched her while Da Costa, all legs and arms, sitting in an arm-chair, as if his limbs had been thrown there without arrangement, and Cortney, very upright on an embroidered stool, talked of the bridge tournament that someone was organising and about which they wanted Ortrud to give advice. At last she handed both of them a pencil and some paper and said:

'Come. Write down the names, each of you, and then compare.'

Lushington was standing apart, examining some of the bric-à-brac that hung about the room. She turned from the others, leaving them writing, and came across the room to him. She spoke to him quickly so that they could not hear. Lushington said:

'Yes. Come to tea tomorrow. To the hotel. I have a sitting-room.'

'You want me to?'

'Of course I want you to.'

'You have thought of me, yes?'

'Yes.'

From the other end of the room Cortney said:

'Frau Mavrin, you'll have to help us with this little problem. The two best players in town have both been divorced from the third best. How is this going to affect the tourney?'

They discussed the problem. The wooden clock on the mantelpiece struck and the cuckoo appeared noisily. Da Costa and Cortney both looked at their watches and began to get up. Ortrud said:

'But you must not go yet.'

'You forget, Frau Mavrin, the affairs of state. The councils of Europe.'

'Then I must see all of you again soon.'

Cortney kissed her hand. Da Costa did not; so Lushington did not do so either. She opened the door of the flat.

'You can work the lift?' she said.

'We will walk,' said Da Costa. 'It is only a few flights.'

'It is easy to work.'

'No, no,' said Cortney. 'We will walk.'

Just as they were leaving the flat the other door of the room they had been in opened and the Professor appeared. He was wearing full evening dress, and when he saw that the guests were going home he threw up his hands.

'Ach, gentlemen——'

'Panteleimon, you are too late. What could have kept you so long?'

'My dear wife——'

'My poor Panteleimon, you have had this trouble and now our guests are departing. I have been the cause of all your trouble.'

'It is no trouble, my dear Ortrud. Only I am sorry that we lose our guests. But wait, I will take them down in the lift.'

'No, no, Professor Mavrin,' said Da Costa. 'We couldn't allow that. Not for one moment. We will certainly walk.'

Cortney said: 'Professor, we have abused your hospitality enough for one night. You go right back to bed. Don't you go near that elevator.'

'I insist, gentlemen, I insist,' said the Professor and, herding them into the lift, pressed the button.

They reached the hall in safety, although the lift stopped about a foot from the floor and they had to open the gates and jump the rest of the way to the ground. As this position seemed final the Professor shook them by the hand and returned to his home by the stairs. Cortney said:

'Well, here I leave you, as my own apartment is just two blocks from this spot.'

They said good-night to him. It was snowing a little. As they walked towards a drosky Da Costa said to Lushington:

'I thought you were rather offhand with Frau Mavrin. Did you have a quarrel with her on the boat? Or is that just your way with women?'

13

LYING in bed in his room at the hotel in a dry blackness of heavy curtains and radiators and with a bulk of untucked-in bedclothes continually slipping off him, Lushington considered, through his trance of early morning dozing, whether or not he had behaved wisely the night before. He had come to no conclusions when someone opened the door and turned on the electric light. The glare of the lamp was an agony, so that he shut his eyes again, but not before he had seen that it was a fair wizened man who had come into the room.

'Who are you?' said Lushington, still with his eyes shut.

'I'm Pope, sir. Mr. Da Costa's man. I expect Mr. Da Costa mentioned I was going to call you.'

He coughed behind his hand. Lushington tried to adjust his memory. The man's face was certainly familiar, so he said:

'Oh, yes, he did. But you have called me rather early, haven't you? What is the time?'

'Mr. Da Costa told me to call you first, sir. Mr. Da Costa goes to the chancellery rather late sometimes. He said that he thought it would be better if I called you first. Those were his orders.'

'By all means call me first. Very likely Mr. Da Costa does not get up until lunch. But is it necessary to be as early as this? This is an unearthly hour.'

'I'm afraid it would be *very inconvenient* to call you at any other time, sir. I am sorry.'

69

Pope's eyes narrowed. He looked for a moment, rather wistfully, at Lushington lying in bed, as if he were sorry for anyone who had fallen so low. Then he turned away and drew up the blinds. It was still dark outside. Central heating pervaded the room and Lushington's skin felt parched. He lay in bed wondering how expensive the employment of Pope was going to be. He said:

'I suppose it would be dangerous to sleep with one of the windows open?'

'Very dangerous. I did it once myself when I first came out here and they thought I was going to die. The doctors despaired of me. There were three doctors and they all despaired of me. One of them was a very famous specialist out here. A man with a big reputation. Which suit will you wear, sir?'

'The blue one.'

'The one you wore yesterday?'

'Yes.'

Pope hesitated. He said:

'If you did not wear the suit you wore yesterday, sir, I could brush it.'

'All right; I'll wear the other one.'

'The brown one?'

'Yes.'

'The brown one needs pressing terribly, sir.'

'I know.'

'Shall I press it for you, sir?'

'Will you?'

Uneasily Pope watched Lushington in bed. He said:

'Would it be better if you wore the blue suit today and then I can press the brown one? Would that be convenient?'

'Yes, yes, I'll do that.'

Lushington turned over with his face towards the wall

and thought about Ortrud. He felt certain that he was getting into a mess. He tried to will Pope to go out of the room and leave him in peace. From behind him he heard Pope clear gently his throat and say:

'I believe I saw you at Maxim's last night, sir?'

'I was there. I did not see you.'

'I was in the gallery, sir. I do not go there often. To speak the truth, I do not find it a very good entertainment. But I am afraid I am very pleasure-loving by nature. Any gaiety has always appealed to me.'

'Has it?'

'They have a curious custom here,' Pope said. 'In a public place you may ask a lady to dance with you before you have been introduced to her. It took me a long time to get used to that. What tie will you wear, sir?'

'Any tie.'

'The grey one?'

'Yes. The grey one.'

'Or this one, sir?'

'The grey one.'

'Would this one go better with the brown suit?'

'All right, that one.'

'Of course it's a custom that widens your acquaintance a great deal,' Pope said. 'There's no doubt about that, whatever one may feel about the etiquette. But then I like society. I only feel at ease when I am with people. My own family have often remarked on it.'

'Have they?'

'They call me the Duke. Jokingly, of course.'

Lushington said nothing because he was still feeling sleepy and could at that moment think of nothing apposite to say. Pope made a clicking noise with his tongue. He said:

'I'm sorry, sir. You said that you would wear the blue

suit and not the brown one. In that case you will like to wear the grey tie after all. They would go together better.'

'Yes, if you think so.'

'And what shirt, sir?'

'The same shirt.'

'It is rather soiled, sir.'

Lushington said: 'I know it is. I like it like that.'

He turned over again and began to doze, abandoning all effort to wake up. He had begun to dream when he felt Pope touch his shoulder and shake him slightly. Not hard, but enough to make him feel a little sick.

'What is it?'

'You won't go to sleep again, sir, will you?'

14

ALTHOUGH the snow had come the cold was not excessive. The snow lay on the spires and the red railway station and on the timber warehouses down by the harbour. Lushington used to sit in his room in the hotel and write articles in the morning, going out before lunch to send telegrams to the paper. He found the atmosphere congenial to writing articles about London as if he were still living there. The telegrams were for the most part about communist organisations or anti-communist organisations, according to his mood. These people were having trouble with the Communists and also with the Agrarians and the National Party and the Social-Democrats and the Fascists and more recently with the Jews and Jesuits, so that there was always plenty to telegraph home about and Lushington used to send long expensive cables to the paper which subsequently appeared in two lines, low on the page opposite the sporting news. In the afternoon he collected information. Everyone he met was anxious to give him as much information as possible in order that matters should be reported from their point of view, except Da Costa, who, suddenly seized with a fear that he appeared unimportant, assumed an air of secrecy about affairs of state as soon as he and Lushington were alone together, which happened usually for not less than two hours every day. In public, however, when thinking of other things, he would divulge any information that might be required of him. When Da Costa became secretive Lushington as a reprisal talked about Lucy, and also to work off his own feelings about her, which, as he now saw Ortrud several times a week, had become quite complex. One or two letters arrived from Lucy telling him what to tell Da Costa about herself.

So the days passed.

In the evening there were usually dinner-parties given by members of the Diplomatic Corps or persons connected in some way with the Government. When there were no dinner-parties Lushington went to the cinema with Ortrud or played piquet with Da Costa. But there were invitations to dinner most nights and dances or parties quite often as well. The dinner-parties began early and ended late, but it was possible to feel ready for them when the evening came by spending some of the afternoon walking among the pine forests along the shore.

15

BARONESS PUCKLER'S parties were in no way different from those given by members of the Diplomatic Corps. Her husband as a young man had in fact been in the Service (of which country no one seemed to remember) although he was retired when, a few years before the War, he had been killed motor-racing in France. Baroness Puckler continued to keep up her foreign connections when she returned home, and the circumstance that the province in which she lived had now become a sovereign state was some consolation for the confiscation by its Government of most of her money and all her land, because it provided her at the same time with diplomats to entertain. She lived a quiet life, existing on the memories of dinner conversations she had had twenty years before with Bülow or de Soveral, and she kept even her affection for Ortrud within disciplined bounds. The society to which she had been brought up had been taken away from her and destroyed, but in its place she had constructed a neat miniature world from which she had found it possible to exclude some of the more glaring defects of the great capitals.

That night Lushington found that he was sitting between Madame Theviot, the wife of the French Minister, and a woman whose name he had been unable to catch who was one of the female members of the House of Deputies. Professor Mavrin had been placed opposite and immediately facing him. Out of the corner of his eye he could see

Ortrud at the other end of the table. The female Deputy was talking:

'We are only a little country. A little new country. You must not be surprised if sometimes we do not seem to do things so well as you big countries who have been big countries for so long. You big countries do not know what it is like to be a little country. We are not used to being even a little country yet. You big countries do all the things so well that we little countries do not so well do yet.'

'Oh, but I am sure that you do. You seem to me to do everything so much better than in the big countries. That is why I enjoy being here so much.'

'Ah, you are too kind. You flatter.'

'Not a bit. Not a bit.'

'Yet it is indeed true that here people are interested in culture and education. We are, I am afraid, what in England you would call highbrows. We must always be modern. Up-to-date. We read Shaw and Wilde. Barrie we find too sentimental.'

'Quite.'

'You see I tell you that you may understand our point of view. We must always, as you say, go ahead. We cannot remain inactive. We must move.'

'Exactly.'

On the other side of him Madame Theviot was examining with her fork the food that had been put in front of her. She was a woman of great height, who was accustomed to wear a turban which hinted of Madame Tallien and hot moments under the *Directoire,* while at the same time it diminished in no way the dignity inherent in French official life. She came from Rennes and almost all the fun she got out of life was being rude to the German Minister, whose surname happened to be of some international significance. She also enjoyed bullying her husband. The female Deputy continued:

'You have seen that they play the *Loyalties* of Galsworthy at the National Theatre?'

She leaned across Lushington and said to Madame Theviot:

'*Vous en avez vu, Madame? Le* Loyalties *de Galsworthy au Théâtre National?*'

Madame Theviot paused, the fork at her lips. She looked suspiciously at the female Deputy and said:

'*Eh bien, qu'est-ce que c'est que ça, Madame?*'

The female Deputy said: '*Dites à Madame de quoi il s'agit.*'

Lushington said: '*C'est un officier anglais qui est très brave et qui volait cinq cents livres d'un juif qui reste à la même maison dans la campagne. L'officier a sauté dans la chambre à coucher du juif par la fenêtre quand celui-là est au salle de bain. Il est découvert parce que la veille il a sauté également sur la bibliothèque du fumoir.*'

'*Hein?*'

'*Et puis le juif est chassé de son cercle par les anciens camarades de l'école du capitaine, qui se tue lui-même.*'

'*Aaah,*' said Madame Theviot, nodding her head with recollections of the Dreyfus case.

'*En effet,*' said the female Deputy. '*C'est une spectacle magnifique. Voilà six fois que je l'ai vue.*' She turned again to Lushington and said: 'And what in England are they thinking about the Expressionism?'

'They find it much too subjective,' Lushington said firmly.

Professor Mavrin from his chair opposite said:

'I look forward to talking to you of English literature at some time more than hitherto we have had the opportunity, Mr. Lushington. I tell my wife to invite you. Always it

seems that she forgets or you cannot come. It is my wish
to discuss with you the novels of Thomas Hardy and his
belief in the inevitability of circumstances. We will have
a long talk one day on that subject. We will choose a
time when we have many hours before us.'

The Professor stroked his moustache and repeated the
words 'many hours' to himself. He had a sallow face with
several lines across the forehead. During the Revolution he
had been frequently shot at, and in the end had almost
starved to death. He was deflected from Thomas Hardy by
the girl on his left, the daughter of one of the judges of the
Supreme Court, who began a conversation with him on
the subject of proportional representation. Baroness Puckler
said:

'You must stay, Mr. Lushington, for the ball at the House
of the Knights. It is next month and is a great occasion.'

'I shall certainly stay for it. I have heard so much about
it that I shall stay even if I am ordered to go back before it
takes place.'

Baroness Puckler said: 'And this year, Colonel, will you
join in the mazurka?'

The British military attaché, an obese sapper, who had
left his wife and large family in rooms at Camberley, said
coquettishly:

'I hope that at least I shall have the pleasure of a waltz
with you, Baroness.'

'We shall see. Perhaps I shall dance with General Kuno
all the evening.'

Da Costa, who was sitting on the other side of Madame
Theviot and who had been engaged in telling her a long
story about his experiences at a spiritualist séance at
Dresden, where he had once lived with a German family,
now turned his attention to the rest of the conversation and
said at the top of his voice:

'Haven't you heard that Madame Mavrin and I are going to give an exhibition dance at the ball this year—a new form of the tango—in Argentine national dress? I'm having my spurs specially sharpened for it.'

Professor Mavrin said: 'Mr. Da Costa, my wife has told me nothing of this. My dear Ortrud, have you made arrangements to hire the suitable costume? You must not leave it too late, because you know how difficult it is sometimes to procure in this small city such things as fancy dress.'

Ortrud, who was sitting at the other end of the table next to the female Deputy's husband, who was a dentist and said to be very talented, said:

'But, Panteleimon, Mr. Da Costa is not serious——'

'But, my dear Ortrud, I should be delighted for you to take part in such a display. I should not mind at all. It would please me very much and I am sure that you would sustain such a role with great distinction.'

'After that,' said Da Costa, who was laughing convulsively to himself at his own humour, 'after that, General Kuno and I are going to give an exhibition of step-dancing, only each of us will wear the other's clothes.'

'Impossible!' said Professor Mavrin. 'Impossible! No, no! Mr. Da Costa, we cannot believe that——'

'Speaking of General Kuno,' said the military attaché, who disliked Da Costa and considered that he had already gone too far, 'I hear that two men were arrested last night in his house. They had broken in and it is thought that they were assassins.'

Professor Mavrin said: 'And only a few months ago such a thing happened before. In the end someone will murder him.'

Baroness Puckler said: 'No. Now, I do not think so. So often they have tried in the past and always they have

79

failed. They have derailed trains he was travelling in. They have thrown bombs at him. They have shot at him from behind walls. But always he escapes. I think he will die quietly in his bed at a great age.'

'Why do they try to kill General Kuno?' Lushington said.

Baroness Puckler said: 'During the troubles he shot many Bolsheviks. Many, many Bolsheviks. Once he made a mistake and shot a great lot of men who were not Bolsheviks. There were many hundreds of them. In those days it was hard to tell. Therefore he has enemies. He is head of the police too. That may cause him to be disliked by some persons.'

16

POPE always found difficulty in leaving a room expediti-
ously. Undisciplined, he gave out vitality in such wrong
directions as Da Costa with enormous force. But this
electric activity was instantly dissipated on reaching its goal
because, strangely, Da Costa possessed against it some effortless resisting power. It was a process comparable to the
pouring of liquid on to an inverted vessel. The whole room
would be messed up with Pope's personality and Da Costa
alone would remain untouched. A certain awareness of this
made Da Costa prefer Pope to any other subordinate that he
had ever known, because through him he became conscious
of a sense of power that was rare to him. By Pope his own
life was made fuller.

At the moment Pope was making preparations for
leaving the flat, delaying the final exit, hovering, toying
with the past. He said:

'For example, an amusing thing happened to my grand-
parents. When they were driving to their wedding the
bottom of the cab—one of those old-fashioned growlers,
I suppose it was—fell out and they had to run all the way
to the church. The cabman was deaf, you see. They
couldn't make him hear. They had to run all the way. It
was a ridiculous thing to happen. The story is often told in
my family. We often laugh over it. It's funny, don't you
think?'

Lushington and Da Costa agreed that it was funny. Pope
shook his head and laughed. There was a silence. The

noise of the trams, clanging along ringing their bells, came up from the street below.

'Funny things like that are always happening in my family,' Pope said.

He watched them for a few moments and then backed with reluctance through the door. They heard him fiddling about with the coats in the hall. Da Costa lit a cigarette. He said:

'He's an amusing fellow—Pope—don't you think?"

'Oh, yes, he is.'

'I don't think he talks too much, do you?'

'Not a bit.'

They looked down at the town's jutting-out pieces of grey masonry and the steeples which Pope, when speaking to Da Costa or anyone else with whom the simile would be likely to bear weight, was accustomed to compare to the dreaming spires of Oxford. There was in fact a distinct resemblance. Lushington said:

'Well, I must be going. I have an appointment.'

'Something nice?'

'Yes.'

'You're lucky. I suppose you've got hold of some woman. Don't get involved in a scandal or everybody will blame me.'

'All right. I'll be careful.'

'And don't forget that we are both dining with Cortney tomorrow night. Black tie. If you forget he'll think I never gave you the message.'

'I won't forget.'

'Oh, and I meant to ask you. Have you heard from Lucy lately? How is she?'

'I had a postcard a couple of days ago. She seemed well. Sent her love.'

'I must write to her,' Da Costa said.

17

THEY used to lunch together at a little Hungarian restaurant down by the quays where the plat de jour was either *goulash esterhazy* or *bœuf stroganoff,* though it was always possible, as a change, to eat *wiener schnitzel.* They sat in one of the cramped wooden partitions into which the room was divided. It was customary to begin the meal with *bouillon.* Ortrud sat next to the wall. Lushington said:

'Where does your husband lunch?'

'At the Café Weber.'

'Every day?'

'Yes.'

'Does he never come here?'

'Of course not.'

'Why not?'

'Because he always lunches at the Café Weber.'

Then one day the Professor arrived. They had just finished their *boullion.* The Professor, who was short-sighted, sat down at the next table without noticing them and began to order his food. Ortrud leaned across:

'Why, Panteleimon, whatever are you doing here?'

'Ach, Ortrud——'

'Remember to talk English. Mr. Lushington does not understand our language.'

The Professor said: 'It is a great pleasure to see you both here. But, my dear wife, today you said you were taking the midday meal with Frau Koski. You have not by chance forgotten your engagement with Frau Koski?'

'Frau Koski telephoned to put off that engagement. I met Mr. Lushington in the street.'

'Your wife was kind enough to accept an invitation to lunch.'

'Too kind, too kind,' said the Professor. 'But now you must both lunch with me. Yes, yes, I insist. Not one word. Mr. Lushington, I invite you to lunch with me and I insist that you accept.'

'Panteleimon, why do you take lunch here today?'

'The Café Weber was so crowded when I entered it.'

'Indeed?'

'And then I have a slight *migraine*. I could not tolerate the noise.'

Lushington ate his *goulash* and said:

'Well, it's very nice that you have decided to come here instead.'

The Professor had a light lunch of ham and gherkins. He seemed tired, but he was in splendid form otherwise and questioned Lushington about the history of the sonnet sequence in English literature. It was one of the Professor's outstanding merits that he rarely spoke of his own subject, psychology. He had some coffee after the ham and then said that he must go back to the University to work. Ortrud said:

'This afternoon, my dear husband, I shall spend shopping.'

The Professor went away and Lushington and Ortrud continued their lunch. When they had finished they went to a cinema and watched a neatly-put-together film dealing with American lower middle-class life. The story, which was credible without being convincing, described the difficulties of a man, a super-excellent dancer, who knew that he could not win the local dancing competition if he danced with his wife, because she was so pure that, as a girl, she had never been taught to dance at all and had evidently been unable to pick up the knack in later life. Since it was imperative that he should win the prize in order to pay for the baby she was about to give birth to he entered for the competition with a blonde girl of indifferent morals. The plot hinged on the arrival of his wife at the critical point of the competition and her swooning away at the degrading sight. A certain air of mystery was added to this drama of domestic relationships by the fact that it had been written as a talkie and was now being played as a silent film with a few captions. When this entertainment was at an end Lushington walked back with Ortrud towards her home. On the way there, turning the corner of some government buildings, they met the Professor again. Ortrud said: 'Panteleimon, are you going home so soon?'

'My headache. I go home to lie down for a little. Remember that we have an invitation to dinner tonight.'

'Mr. Lushington was kind and took me to the films.'

'He is too good to you. Mr. Lushington, you are too kind to my wife.'

Lushington walked with them as far as their flat. Then he went back to the hotel to change for dinner. He found Pope sitting at his table writing letters. He dislodged him and began to change. He was dining that night with the Danish first secretary.

He arrived a few minutes too early for dinner, although Cortney was already standing in front of the fire, fingering a new sort of white tie which had arrived for him from London the day before. Their hostess, a little Danish countess, who looked like a squirrel, said:

'The Mavrins are coming tonight, Mr. Lushington. You have met them?'

'Yes, I have met them. As it happens, I saw them this afternoon.'

'She is so charming, do not you think?'

'Yes, indeed.'

Cortney said: 'Mr. Lushington was fortunate enough to travel here on the same boat as Madame Mavrin.'

'*So?* And he fell in love with her, of course? I am sure you did. Is not that true?'

'But of course.'

'Now, Countess,' said Cortney, 'remember you mustn't make jokes like that in the presence of someone who comes from the New World, where we still try to retain our homely code of morals. In the first place we don't understand them.'

'And then Mr. Da Costa is coming from your legation. I expect you see him sometimes?'

'Yes,' said Lushington, 'I do see him quite often as a matter of fact.'

'To speak of morals,' said their host, 'have you heard the latest story about Madame Gomez?'

It was a good one. Later the Mavrins arrived and the Swedish naval attaché and the daughters of the German Minister, and Da Costa, rather late. After dinner they danced to the wireless, except Professor Mavrin, who talked with their host about the economics of farming, the collectivist system in Russia, and the methods that obtained in Denmark. Da Costa was in one of his noisy moods and he danced most of the time with Ortrud. Lushington watched her, thin and exotic in one of her exaggerated dresses. He wondered if she was a serious person.

18

LUSHINGTON had been lunching at Da Costa's flat and they were sitting there drinking coffee. As usual the room was too hot. Lunch, cooked by Pope, had been good and, while eating it, they had talked about their friends in London and both had now been left with an inevitable sense of being cut off, outposts of a mighty empire, pleasant in a way but melancholy, and now they sat in silence smoking. Da Costa said:

'I don't think Bellamy ought to call me a bloody fool. It is not so much that I care whether or not he should think that I am one, as the appalling want of dignity it argues in a man of his age and rank in the service. I mean, if he can't learn to control his temper how on earth can he hope to control the fate of nations?'

'Of course his repressions are something awful,' Lushington said.

'That may be. But if he represses his evil desires he ought to repress his temper as well. After all, from the point of view of working with him in the legation, it would be much better if it were the other way about. And by the same token I thought it very impertinent of old Mavrin to tell Bellamy that Madame Mavrin was free for dinner on Tuesday without consulting you first.'

'What on earth do you mean?'

'Nothing.'

'Anyway,' said Lushington, 'she's not going to dine with the Bellamys on Tuesday. She is going to dine with me.'

'In that case you have supplied the answer to your own question. And now I must go away and do some work.'

'May I stay here and write?'

'Of course.'

Da Costa went away and Lushington settled down to writing articles. He opened one of the windows so that an icy shaft of air blew across one side of the room. He had worked for some time before he noticed that Pope was in the room too. Pope made his presence known by shutting the window and bolting it. After becoming aware of Pope's arrival Lushington continued to write for a little time although he knew that it would be no good. With Pope in the room he could not hope to compose a sentence. Pope crept round by the walls, touching everything. Lushington listened to his movements and at last gave up all effort to work. He pushed back his chair and said to Pope:

'It seems a pity to stay in on a lovely day like this, although it is a bit cold, and so I think I shall go out for a walk.'

He said this although he knew that he was going back to his hotel as quickly as possible so that he might be able to go on writing there. Pope put himself in an attitude of conversation. He said:

'When it is warmer, sir, I always get into shorts after finishing my work and run in the outlying districts of the town. I find it is absolutely necessary for my health. I am not by any means a strong man. I have to take care of my health, and exercise is an absolute necessity. It used to give rise to a great deal of comment when I first came out here. Now, however, people seem to have become more accustomed to it. I once suggested to Mr. Da Costa that he should do the same when he complained to me of a heavy feeling.'

'Did he take your advice?'

88

'No, sir. He did not.'

'I'm not surprised to hear that he did not.'

'Mr. Da Costa is a strange gentleman, if you don't mind my saying so, sir.'

'Why?' said Lushington.

He disliked the idea of prolonging the conversation with Pope but at the same time felt himself unable to resist possible intimate revelations about so old a friend.

'He spends all his time reading,' Pope said.

He shuddered. Expectantly, Lushington said:

'He has always read a good deal. Ever since I have known him.'

'Curious books, sir.'

'Are they?'

'I'm a great reader myself,' Pope said. 'I always have been. But it doesn't *do* to read too much. Otherwise you don't have a healthy mind in a healthy body.'

'I suppose not.'

'I like reading serious books, sir. Books that really teach you something. Books on economics especially. Science. Statistics. Nature study.'

'Yes, yes,' said Lushington.

A straight talk on Pope's literary tastes had been just what he had wanted to avoid, but self-respect prevented him from returning of his own accord to the subject of Da Costa's vagaries. Pope stood, resting his hands on the table, staring in front of him with his eyes-that-look-beyond-the-grave expression. He had got started. He rapidly sketched in the plots of a few books he had enjoyed during the previous eighteen months.

'Yes . . .' said Lushington, '. . . yes . . . yes . . . yes . . . yes . . . yes. . . .'

Art and letters exhausted, Pope began to roam among the litter of his personal reminiscence, exploring the cramped

G

furtive lanes of memory, winding this way and that through the tinsel by-ways of his past, petting and cosseting his ego, warming it at the glow of innumerable self-congratulatory episodes that had, it seemed, lighted the road. Lushington, realising now that he would hear nothing of Da Costa's secret life, contented himself with the thought that anyway it was probably *The Golden Bough,* merely, that Da Costa spent most of his time reading, and he no longer paid attention to the humming cadences of Pope's saga. Instead he listened to the roll of drums that was sounding from the President's palace, where they were changing the guard. Pope pursued his course:

'. . . during the War when I was in the Army, attached, as it happened, to the Dental Department, one of the officers had remarked that I was good with my hands, he used to say that no one was any use to him after he had employed me, somehow it had spoiled him, he used to say, for other orderlies with their coarse ways, clumsy blighters, jokingly, he used to call them. . . . I can remember that at one time I went into the canteen wearing a mackintosh over my uniform and as soon as I spoke two privates who were sitting there sprang to attention. They literally *sprang* to attention. Curious, wasn't it? Don't you think that it was curious, sir?'

'Yes . . . yes,' said Lushington, lost in speculations of his own.

'There it was,' said Pope, "there it was. You know, sir, at that time my cheeks used to be as red as cherries. Someone once said that I looked the healthiest man in the battalion. He said it wouldn't be going too far to say so. That was during the War, sir. Later when I came out here . . .'

Led by his train of thought to more immediate problems, Lushington waited for an appropriate break in the cascade of anamnesis and then, like the boy thrusting his hand into the hole in the dyke, stemmed the flood by saying:

'And by the way I must not forget to mention to you about those evening shirts of mine. They are ruined. All frayed. Isn't there anywhere here where they can wash stiff shirts?'

'Nowhere, sir, nowhere. Curiously enough, I was just about to tell you that. When I first came out here I thought that I should be forced to wear a false front. You won't believe, but I did indeed. A *dickey*, I think it is called. But then, of course, I find that the majority of my friends here, being foreigners, do not change for dinner every night, so that in the end I found that by constant complaint the laundry managed a little better. That is the only way, I fear, sir. Positively the only way.'

Lushington gathered up his belongings and began to put on his overcoat. Pope helped him on with this with such energy that he was almost pushed off his balance.

'The usual time tomorrow morning, sir?'

'The usual time.'

'Good-afternoon, sir.'

'Good-afternoon.'

As Lushington left the room he saw that Pope was beginning to rearrange the invitation cards on the mantel-piece. He went downstairs and out into the square. A squadron of Waldemar's uhlans were passing, picking the way between the market stalls, most of which were stocked with holly and stunted Christmas trees. The soldiers were on cobby horses and wore short, heavy overcoats bordered with sheepskin. Lushington, standing on the pavement, watched them walk their horses through the slush and then disappear in the traffic at the end of the square. The pennons of their lances flickered above the tops of the trams. Then they were gone as the riders turned the corner into another street. He heard someone behind him say:

'I too might have ridden at the head of a troop of cavalry. But I have few regrets.'

Turning, he found that Count Scherbatcheff was standing beside him. The Count was wearing an astrakhan cap instead of his *béret* and he looked even more haggard than he had done on the voyage. His overcoat hung on him quite loosely as if it were suspended from a hook somewhere beneath his neck. His pale blue eyes were sunk far back into his head.

'Come with me a little way. I am going back to my apartment. I know that Englishmen like a walk.'

'Certainly.'

'You will do so?'

'I should like to very much.'

19

THEY went across the square and down steps towards the river, which they crossed by the Nikolai bridge, walking sharply because the air was cold. On the other side of the river was the poorer part of the town. They passed through this quarter and beyond it, while Count Scherbatcheff told Lushington about his cough and stomach trouble, both of which were worse. He had tried various remedies but none seemed to do him any good. He had hoped that in this climate he would feel better, but, on the contrary, he was worse here than he had been in Belgium. A nondescript outlying district was now reached. This end of the city, not yet completed, was full of tin huts and the shells of unfinished modern buildings. Sometimes they passed piles of empty petrol tins and stacks of bricks. All this was part of an ambitious town-planning scheme. Then they came to an immense block of flats only half of which had been built, the right-hand wing being nothing but girders, although work seemed to have been abandoned on it, for these were rusty and some of the masonry was already falling away. They seemed to be making their way among the ruins of another civilisation, now passed away, and of which there would soon be no trace. Count Scherbatcheff stopped in front of the completed wing of the flats and said:

'You will come up for a short time? I should be delighted if you would do so and then we could talk for a little longer.'

They went into the hall, which was full of ladders and

pails of whitewash and, as there was a notice on the lift saying that it was out of order, they walked up the stairs to the Scherbatcheff flat, which was on the top floor. Count Scherbatcheff took a key from under the doormat, opened the door and pushed Lushington in front of him into a room which opened directly on to the landing without any hall or passage. The room was in semi-darkness and several people were sitting in it.

Lushington saw that there was an upright piano along one wall at which a girl of about twelve years old with two long plaits down her back was practising scales. She took no notice of their arrival and continued methodically. Two women were sewing in one corner of the room and a man with a yellow shaved head, wearing a grey military overcoat, turned back showing its red lining, was sitting on a kitchen chair and looking out of the window. He did not turn round at their entry, so that Lushington could not tell at all how old he was. In another corner a very old woman was propped up in a chair with a shawl over her knees. She was wearing spectacles and held a book in her hand, although there was not enough light to read by. The outstanding scent among the several odours of the room was that of musk.

Count Scherbatcheff helped Lushington to take off his overcoat and hung it from a nail that was already supporting the picture of a saint. He pulled forward a settee and said:

'Sit down. Can you give me a cigarette? I cannot offer you one. There are never any cigarettes in this house. If I get any my uncle puts them in his pocket and becomes angry if any of us ask for one. Later we will have some tea.'

He did not introduce Lushington to any of the people in the room. No one took any notice of them. The girl with the plaits changed from scales to five-finger exercises and then stopped and altered the height of the music stool, after which she went on again. Count Scherbatcheff said:

'You will agree that there come moments when a man feels that he can stand no more? I know that you are fortunate. You are English. You have at least a profession which is not too uncongenial. But you will understand how it is sometimes with me?'

Lushington looked into the middle distance of the room where, through the shadows, he could still see a high-light on the glazed surface of the unknown man's head. He wondered whether or not this man was the uncle who always filled his pockets with cigarettes. And then remembering that Count Scherbatcheff required an answer he said something about Russians having lost so much. Count Scherbatcheff said:

'No. It is not that. I used to feel the same when I was in the Corps of Pages. If anything, worse. It is just depression, as you call it. And this damned cough.'

'I can sympathise.'

'And then relations—relations—relations.'

'Yes?'

'You see what I mean?'

One of the reasons why the room was so hot was because brown paper had been pasted over the cracks of the windows. In addition to the main stove of the room a small oil-stove had been placed in the corner near the very old woman. This smaller stove smoked menacingly. The very old woman now shut her book with a snap and, throwing down her rug almost on top of the oil-stove, began to move across the room. Lushington got up to let her pass. Count Scherbatcheff said:

'That is my grandmother about whom I have spoken to you. You remember? Her obstinacy. But do not be alarmed. She speaks little English and besides she is deaf. There is no need for discretion. As I was saying to you, at times matters are indeed impossible.'

'Can I help?'

'As you know, I am an engineer. But what have I to look forward to as an engineer? Shall I live for ever with these people in this room? Yet when I was young and was to enter the Chevalier Guards I was the same. I thought always of the interminable round of tiresome social engagements and the tedious duties of regimental life that were before me. I could see no way out. I tell you this that you may understand that it is not merely my adversity that causes these sentiments.'

'Anything special at the moment?'

'Yes,' said Count Scherbatcheff. 'Perhaps it is something special. I have been feeling it more than usual. For a longer time. I will tell you. It is Madame Mavrin.'

'What about her?'

'I have thought of her ever since we were together on board the ship. It is impossible for me to see her. What can I do if I did see her? It is clear that she does not like me. That is one of the reasons why I feel as I do.'

'Certainly that makes things difficult.'

Now that his eyes had become accustomed to the half-light Lushington saw that a young man was lying at full length on the ground immediately under the window and in front of the man with the shaved head. This young man was writing in an exercise book by the light thrown by the oil-stove. He was writing lethargically with a stumpy pencil. The girl at the piano still played her five-finger exercises. Count Scherbatcheff said:

'I am aware that in England there exists a somewhat rigid code of morals. But we Russians cannot be bound by convention. It may seem shocking to you that I speak thus of a

96

lady who is already married to another. But at least you will sympathise with me in my despair.'

'Of course.'

'May I ask, do you often meet Madame Mavrin in society? That society from which you know we Russians are, for political reasons, excluded?'

'Quite often.'

'You will perhaps remind her of my existence? That is all I ask.'

'I will certainly tell her that I have seen you.'

'A thousand thanks,' Count Scherbatcheff said, 'a thousand thanks, my dear Lushington. And now I will weary you no more with my troubles. After all, how much more fortunate we are than many. At least we have comfortable quarters. *Enfin,* it is not the Scherbatcheff Palace in Petersburg, but that house was more draughty than any other that I have known and its rooms were for ever full of relations whom I disliked. Here at least are only those whom I can tolerate and even feel affection for.'

The very old woman now returned leading with her by the hand two small children. These she put between the oil-stove and the wall and opening a cupboard brought out some toys, a tin trumpet and a drum which she gave them. Suddenly the young man who was lying on the floor raised himself to his knees. He banged on his exercise book and shouted at the very old woman. She turned towards him and an altercation began. One of the other women stopped her sewing and in a drawling, metallic voice joined the discussion. The children took no notice and began to play in an appropriate manner with their toys. Count Scherbatcheff shrugged his shoulders and looked at Lushington. He said:

'I can only apologise to you as my guest for this disturbance. It is my cousin. He always complains that he cannot work when the children play. Like all the rest of my family he will not listen to the voice of reason. He provokes all of us. Work indeed! He is only learning shorthand. He seems to think that a sufficient reason for imposing his will on all of us.'

The controversy ended at last, the student of shorthand worn down in the last resort by the girl with the plaits, who had now returned to scales. The young man lay down once more on the floor, breathing heavily, sometimes staring and pointing in the direction of the children. Count Scherbatcheff took a bottle of something that he said was good for his cough and poured a few drops on his handkerchief. It smelt potent and Lushington refused it when it was offered to him. Count Scherbatcheff said:

'You will accept a little refreshment? We have no cigarettes, but at least you will join us in a little refreshment. No, you must not refuse. I insist. My grandmother will prepare something. I will ask her to do so at once.'

He went across the room to where his grandmother was sitting and shouted in her ear. She shook her head and he shouted again. Once more she shook her head. The noise of the Count's shouting was broken at intervals by the piano and more fitfully by the trumpet. The child with the drum had at last succeeded in forcing one of the drumsticks through the parchment and was laboriously enlarging by hand the hole. Count Scherbatcheff came back to the settee. He said:

'She is hopeless. Hopeless. I ask her to prepare a simple meal for my guest and she at once makes difficulties. We have not got this, we have not got that, we have not got the other. *Toujours les histoires de cuisine.*'

'But——'

'Please. Please, my dear Lushington, that is enough. We may be exiles and in difficult circumstances, but at least we have not forgotten the name of hospitality. Ah, why do we

98

live in this accursed country? How could such a situation as this arise in a civilised capital like Paris, London or New York? You will agree that matters have gone a little far when this happens?'

'Really——'

Count Scherbatcheff pushed aside the table so that it came into contact with the end of the piano and knocked some of the books of music from the top of it. This rearrangement of the furniture gave him access to a small door with panels of frosted glass. He opened this door and shouted:

'Katya! Katya!'

Through the door there was a room, a little larger than a telephone box, with a sink at one end of it. In front of the sink an old woman, less old than Count Scherbatcheff's grandmother, but at the same time quite old, was asleep in an upright chair. She wore large carpet slippers and had a handkerchief tied round her head. Count Scherbatcheff took her arm, waking her. She listened to what he said to her, standing in front of him with her eyes upon the ground and her arms hanging limply on either side of her body. Then she spoke at some length and pointed to a pile of unwashed dishes on the edge of the sink. Count Scherbatcheff said nothing. He held out his hands in an attitude of resignation. Then the old woman began to open the cupboards that were all round her and to take things out of them. Count Scherbatcheff returned. He said:

'Now all will be well. If I cannot rely on my relatives, at least one who has been so long in our service as Katya respects my wishes.'

'But I assure you——'

'Not another word. Besides, I myself am hungry.'

Katya moved the table away from the piano again and pushed it against the settee. Then she cleared a space at one end of it. There were objects of every description on the table and these she put on the top of the piano, that was already piled high with books and music. On the space she cleared she put a plate of chocolate biscuits, some ham, a few pieces of beetroot, a decanter half-full of cherry brandy and a wooden box with a design lacquered on it and with assorted jujubes inside. The grandmother, who had been watching these preparations from her chair, now got up and, again throwing the rug on the floor by the oil-stove, she moved across the room. Lushington wondered if she were about to throw him out neck and crop and if so whether or not the rest of the family would help her. But she spoke quite quietly to Count Scherbatcheff. Again her grandson shouted in her ear. And then she began to smile. Count Scherbatcheff himself laughed. He leaned towards his grandmother and kissed her on the chin. After doing this he turned to Lushington and said:

'It is I who must apologise. My grandmother was not at fault. It is all a ridiculous mistake. My grandmother misunderstood me. She is deaf, as I told you. She supposed that I wished that you should stay with us for several days, sleeping on the chaise-longue. She says that no one may sleep on the chaise-longue until it has been mended. Otherwise it will be broken so that it can never be repaired.'

'But how could she think that I could trespass——'

'Also she supposed that you were a Pole. The Polish consul. She has this prejudice against Poles. But now I have explained clearly who you are. All difficulties are at an end. Indeed if you would like to stay with us for a day or two I have no doubt that the difficulty about the chaise-longue could easily be surmounted.'

Lushington was presented to the grandmother, who joined them in a glass of cherry brandy. Count Scherbatcheff said:

'It sometimes makes me sad to think that her death was foretold in the cards. But that is mortal fate. We must learn to face bereavement. Much is given that much may be taken away.'

Later on in the evening they played ragtimes on the portable gramophone and Lushington and Count Scherbatcheff danced in turn with the girl with the plaits, who was persuaded by the rest of the family to conclude her practising for that day. Even the young man lying on the floor gave up his shorthand notes and listened to the music for a while.

20

DINNER that night at the Mavrins' had not been entirely successful. The Professor was undoubtedly prolix in telling an anecdote which Lushington had heard more than once before and Ortrud was in a bad mood. By a mischance Lushington upset a glass of wine over her dress. It was a night when things were not going well. Professor Mavrin did his best, but clearly he was too used to Ortrud's ways to be more than a little disturbed. They had left the dining-room. The Professor said:

'It seemed to me that of all the ladies last night the Countess Arnhfeldt was the most beautiful.'

Ortrud said: 'My dear Panteleimon, but how absurd! *Chic,* perhaps, but not beautiful. Her face is like that of a rat. She is well dressed like all Danes. That is a national characteristic. But she has no features.'

She stood there, waiting to be contradicted. Lushington said:

'Not at all. I disagree. I think Professor Mavrin is quite right. She seemed to me to be looking lovely.'

'I suppose you find her very attractive?'

'Yes, I do.'

'What a ridiculous thing to say!'

'My dear Ortrud, Mr. Lushington is our guest.'

'But if he says such ridiculous things——'

'It is not ridiculous at all. I entirely agree with the Professor. Surely you are not jealous of her?'

'Jealous of Countess Arnhfeldt——'

'No, of course I know you aren't really. I was only joking. But to the Professor and myself she seemed clearly to be so beautiful.'

'Certainly, my dear Ortrud, Mr. Lushington is right. You must be jealous. But how silly you are, because you yourself are far more beautiful even than Countess Arnhfeldt.'

'You may think so. Mr. Lushington does not.'

'But indeed I do. Why should you think that I do not?'

'At least, my dear, Mr. Lushington has a right to his own opinions on such matters. You will grant me that?'

'A perfect right to such bad taste.'

'Bad taste! To think that you are a more beautiful woman than Countess Arnhfeldt?'

'He does not think it. He only says it. I see by his face that he considers her the more beautiful. What a pity that we did not invite her here tonight.'

'But, my dear Ortrud, you said especially when I suggested that we should invite Frau Koski, whom I knew to be dis-engaged tonight, that you would prefer to have no other guests. I cannot understand why you should now wish that we had invited Countess Arnhfeldt.'

'I say so only because Mr. Lushington seems to find her so attractive.'

'My wife, you are exaggerating in the most absurd manner. There is no reason to suppose that Mr. Lushington has any particular wish to see Countess Arnhfeldt at this moment, although I have no doubt that he admires her as much as we all do.'

'As a matter of fact I should have enjoyed her presence very much indeed,' Lushington said.

'What did I tell you, Panteleimon?'

'My dear Ortrud, moderate your tone.'

'*Sei doch endlich still!* Be silent!'

The Professor rose. He said:

'I shall go to my study and complete my work until you are in a better mood. Alone with our guest you will perhaps be able to control yourself with more decorum than in my presence. Mr. Lushington, you will excuse me?'

He left the room with dignity. When he had gone Lushington said:

'Let one thing be clearly understood. I will not have you speaking to your husband in that way.'

'And why not?'

'Because you should show him some respect. He is a very clever man indeed and you speak to him as if he were a schoolboy.'

'He was in the wrong.'

'He was not in the wrong. And even if he had been, that would have been no excuse.'

'After all he is my husband and not yours.'

'It is because he is your husband that you should treat him with some consideration.'

Ortrud began to dab her eyes with a handkerchief. She said:

'I know that you do not love me. But do not be so unkind. It was all on your account that I was so silly.'

'Well, really?'

'Yes, yes, you know it. Why do you never consider how I feel?'

'Well, don't cry anyway.'

'I am unhappy.'

'Why?'

'Because you don't love me.'

'But I do. I do.'

'Yes? A little?'

'Yes. A lot.'

When the Professor returned everyone was in a better temper.

21

IT was snowing. The flakes were small and those that fell close to the window seemed, as they drifted past, almost black. Flags were flying all over the town because it was Independence Day and that morning there had been a review and the President, standing under the statue of the national poet, had taken the salute of several infantry battalions, a cavalry regiment, some gunner batteries, a few signallers on motor-bicycles, and a tank. Great precautions had been taken to prevent a demonstration on the part of dissatisfied minorities or disgruntled individuals who might be expected to shout rude words or to throw bombs. In the end the President himself was entirely hidden by his suite and plain-clothes men, a fact that was unfavourably commented upon by Baroness Puckler, who said that in the days before the War, when anarchists were an adjunct to any public function of any importance, no royalty would have dreamed of taking so much trouble to remain alive. But she added that she knew that the men of today were of a different mould. Lushington watched the review with her and then came home to write up an account of it. Now he was working while Pope, wearing a tartan tie, stood by the door with one hand on his hip, which protruded as if dislocation had taken place. Pope said:

'I had the privilege of meeting a friend of yours last night, sir. A very nice gentleman. A count.'

'Indeed?'

'Count Bobel his name was.'

'Bobel? Bobel?'

'Bobel, sir.'

As it would be useless at this stage to deny that he had ever heard of such a person, Lushington put down his pen and said:

'Yes. I remember that there was someone of that name on the boat.'

'A very nice gentleman, sir.'

'I did not have the opportunity of seeing much of him.'

'Oh, but he said that he knew you very well indeed, sir.'

'He did? Perhaps he was confusing me with someone else.'

'Oh, no, I don't think so, sir. As it happened, I was able to do him a small service. In the place I met him, it was a species of tavern, and I was there with my fiancée, the Count had forgotten to bring his pocket-book. Both he and the four ladies with him would have been in a very awkward predicament if I had not been enabled to lend the Count a small sum.'

'Much?'

'No, sir. A very trivial amount. But the Count said that, should it happen that he was called away on business unexpectedly, he knew you well enough to be able to say that you would repay me at any time and get the money back from him later, as you would be bound to be seeing him again soon in the not very distant future.'

'He said that, did he?'

'Being a count, sir,' Pope said, 'I took his word. After all, I thought, you can't beat *noblesse oblige*. Not that I myself believe in a system of hereditary titles. I think it a vicious one from start to finish. As a matter of fact I'm a socialist. After all, socialism is bound to come. Bound to. Look at Russia, look at Germany, look at France, look at Italy even——'

Lushington said: 'Before looking at any of these I must

make it clear that in the future and as long as I am in this country I refuse to be held responsible for any debts incurred by anyone whatsoever. Anyone. Not even Mr. Da Costa.'

'Exactly, sir. Exactly. I quite understand. But as I was with my fiancée, who also knows you, I felt that I ought to take the Count's word.'

'But I don't know your fiancée. I didn't know that you possessed one.'

'Miss Flosshilde, sir. The young lady at the reception desk of this hotel. With the auburn hair, sir.'

'Oh.'

'You may know to whom I refer, sir.'

'Yes.'

'We hope to get married next year, sir.'

'Next year? Indeed?'

Pope said: 'When my great-aunt died she expressed a wish that I should take the name of my mother in addition to my own. My mother was a Malpas. It was a wish that I hope will be fulfilled when I get married.'

'Then you will be Malpas-Pope?'

'No, sir. Pope-Malpas. Is there anything else, sir?'

Lushington got up from the table. He said:

'Yes. There is. What have the laundry done to the stiff shirt of mine that came back yesterday? What have they done to it? Or rather I can see what they have done to it, but how have they done it? Why was it ever sent there? Can I get any compensation? Have any more clothes been sent there this week? Is that the only laundry? Or have I got to give up changing for dinner?'

Pope made a gesture with his hands indicative of despair. He shook his head despondently at the same time and, by this movement, dismissed the subject from the sphere of serious discussion. He said:

'You must often have thought it odd that I am not married already, sir. I don't mind telling you it has not been for the want of being asked. You wouldn't believe it, sir, if I were to tell you some of the things that women have said to me. Terrible things. Things that I couldn't speak out loud. Not even to you, sir. But Miss Flosshilde is different. She isn't like that.'

'I'm glad to hear it.'

'When I was last in England,' Pope said, 'I used to take my little nephew, my sister's child, about with me a great deal. You never saw such a fine child. Everyone noticed him. Everyone. They used to stop me in the street or in the park or on buses and trams and say what a lucky man I was to be the father of such a child. Do you know, sir, I used to blush so hotly that they didn't know what they had said to make me go like that? I used to blush all up here.'

'I don't wonder.'

'It was terrible,' Pope said. 'And by the way, sir, I forgot to tell you that Madame Mavrin rang up this afternoon before you had come in.'

'Did she leave a message?'

'No, sir, but I rather think that she was at first under the impression that it was you answering the telephone, because she did not ask to speak to you by name. She just began speaking, thinking, I suppose, sir, that I was you.'

'Did she leave a message?'

'No, sir.'

Pope coughed very discreetly behind his hand. Then he left the room. Lushington sat down again at his writing table and watched the snow driving past the windows while he tried to compose a letter to Lucy. From the bedroom he could hear Pope humming an individual rendering of *Stenka Razin*.

22

THEY had walked out of the town by the road which led along the shore. Where this road ended there were pines and beyond them birch trees and among these stood a small palace, built in temperate baroque. This place, used at present for nothing in particular, was spoken of as a potential state institution for mental defectives. Meanwhile it was deserted, though waste paper had been left about on one of the terraces and someone had taken the trouble to overturn and to dismember a colossal imperial statue in bronze which had formerly stood at the end of a vista of trees. Anatomical remains of this were sinking into the turf of the lawn or lying about among the flower beds. The steps of the terrace in front had been broken in places and not yet repaired. From the top of the steps there was a good view of the town, where wisps of smoke hung round the shapeless citadel. Out to sea a few boats paused or turned, manœuvring to enter the docks. Beyond were the islands where fishermen and professional smugglers lived. The afternoon was sharp and sunny. Ortrud, who was standing at the top of the steps, said:

'The Deputy-Chief of the Air Service is under arrest.'

Lushington was examining the head of the statue, which lay with its heavy Roman nose buried in the grey brittle grass. Contact with the earth had given the potentate's face an agreeable patina. Beside it was an arm and a hand holding an orb. Farther off, an immense top-boot.

'Why?'

'He found a man in his wife's bedroom when he came back last night.'

'Did they put him under arrest for that?'

'He shot the man with his revolver.'

'With his revolver? Did he? That was hasty of him.'

'Honour demanded it.'

'Is the man dead?'

'They say he may recover.'

'I always said that it was dangerous to allow people to walk about in fancy dress armed to the teeth. Now you see what happens.'

'Did you?'

She ran lightly down the steps of the terrace and took his arm. Then, leaning against him, she put one foot on the statue's ear under its wig and tried to rock the head backwards and forwards. It moved slightly, nuzzling into the frozen grass. The broad three-cornered hat had kept the snow from the ground immediately beneath the face.

'Are you in love with me?' she said.

'Of course I am. I'm always telling you I am.'

'More than with the girl you left in England?'

'In a different way.'

'Horrible man.'

She turned away, still holding his arm, leading him up the steps towards the upper terrace. They began to walk round the palace, which was the size of a small English manor house and had been built as a place of retirement from the bustle of court life. There were nymphs holding flower-pots at intervals round the colonnade, but the pots were empty and the glass in most of the windows had been broken. She said:

'I have had other lovers.'

'Have you?'

'Some of them were quite unimportant.'

'I am glad to hear it. Do you count your husband?'

'He is one of the important ones. And you are the most important one of all. Did you know that? That you are the most important one of all?'

The breeze from the sea blew across the gardens and carried some few remnants of leaves, scraps and odds and ends of twigs across the lawn so that they dashed against the tritons and cornucopia of the fountain. Although snow was lying on the roofs of the town, here it was half melted from the grass. Among the beds without flowers and the chipped cupids, the gnawing of actuality seemed for the moment silenced. In this place which had been left without meaning it seemed easier to feel meaning where there was perhaps none. All was very quiet except for an occasional crackling made now and then as birds flew through the trees, or by the bark or branches of the trees themselves.

'What shall I do when I have to go away and leave you?'

'You must not go. I shall come with you. I cannot allow you to go. But why should we talk about that now? Here England is so far away. And you are not going to leave me yet. You are not going to leave me yet, are you?'

'No. Not yet.'

They went up into the woods beyond the garden and along the paths that led inland and upwards, because the palace was in a hollow. The chilly avenues were deserted. Once a peasant passed dragging some wood on a sledge and, with some obscure remembrance of another epoch, touched his cap. The trees swayed about uncertainly. She said:

'You do love me, don't you?'

'Yes. I love you.'

'And I love you?'

'Yes. You love me.'

They walked on between the birch trees.

'And now I must go back,' she said.

'Why?'

'Domestic duties. You forget that I am a wife. I must go back to my home.'

'So soon? Can't we stay here for a bit?'

'No. I must go back.'

They turned down one of the paths which led back towards the sea and brought them to the embankment promenade, a walk that had been fashionable before the Independence. But now that the town had been rebuilt no one came here. Instead the people walked up and down the main boulevard. Only a few soldiers were wandering two-and-two along the embankment, their sheepskin caps and long overcoats making them like the accepted representations of Noah and his children. Ortrud said:

'When you are gone I shall come back to the Little Palace and then I shall be able to remember you.'

'Will you have to go there before you can do that?'

'Of course.'

'And how shall I remember you?'

'I do not know,' she said. 'Perhaps you will remember me when you see your English girl again.'

'But you are coming back with me to England.'

'Oh yes. I forgot.'

He went with her past the barracks as far as the house in the University quarter. When they reached the door he was going to leave her, but she said:

'Come upstairs with me. I cannot say good-bye to you properly in the street.'

The lift was in almost perfect order on that day and they reached their landing in safety. Ortrud opened the door of the flat and Lushington followed her into the hall. From the sitting-room there came a noise of droning, a sort of sing-song, interspersed with high squeaks. The sound was a disagreeable one.

'What is that?'

'Little Panteleimon.'

'Oh?'

'You have not seen him before?'

'No.'

A child of about five years old stood in the middle of the floor of the room, twisting pieces of his clothes in his hands. Little Panteleimon's face was large and round and he stood there, leaning with all his weight on one leg, gazing in front of him with an expression of convinced and dogged cynicism. He watched them as if he were looking through them at something else in the passage beyond.

'Hullo,' said Lushington.

Ortrud spoke to the child in German. Little Panteleimon fixed her with his fishy wide eyes and moved away slightly, crossing one leg behind the other and pointing his toe in the First Position. He was an elderly, world-weary child dressed in the travesty of a sailor suit. He stood there gazing out at them as if through field-glasses. Ortrud said:

'He is shy. Like his father.'

'He looks like his father, curiously enough.'

Ortrud laughed. She went across the room and, taking the child by the hand, kissed him on the forehead.

'Come,' she said. 'Play with this.'

She took Lushington's hat from him and threw it across towards the child. Little Panteleimon did not catch the hat. He stood uncertainly, watching it lying on the floor. Then he moved towards the hat and, pausing for a moment before he picked it up, he began to examine it. Suddenly, very deliberately, he tore off the ribbon that was round it.

'Panteleimon!'

'No, no,' said Lushington. 'It doesn't matter. It's all

right. No one will notice that the ribbon is not sewn on if I put it round the hat to go home in. I can easily wear it like that as far as the hotel.'

Little Panteleimon's face began to quiver. It screwed up. He yelled. Ortrud rang and he was removed by the nurse, a square middle-aged woman wearing peasant costume. Soon through the wall between the rooms they heard him stop yelling. The sounds sank slowly down the scale until they had reached the theme that he had been improvising when they had arrived in the flat and here he remained, keening resolutely. Ortrud said:

'You see I have a family.'

'Yes.'

'So I shall not be able to come with you after all. To come back with you to England. You will have to leave me and go back alone.'

'Yes.'

'Good-bye,' she said, in his arms.

'Good-bye.'

'Mein liebling!'

23

HE walked back through the streets that skirted the University, down past the Institute of Scientific Research, into the central boulevard, crowded at this hour with students in their parti-coloured caps, pacing up and down, seeing life. Some of these were strolling arm-in-arm, making progress difficult. A drosky passed containing Pope and Flosshilde and, seeing Lushington, Pope raised his hat a little way from his head like a royalty and kept it in this position as they drove by. Flosshilde smirked and the sun flashed blindingly on her diamond ring. She was certainly too fat for her age. Lushington, gaping after them, got caught up in a chain of students and was carried some little way in the wrong direction. He reached the hotel at last and went through the swing doors. The lounge was full of people having tea or *aperitifs*. Da Costa and Waldemar were sitting at one of the tables, smoking. When he saw Lushington, Da Costa said:

'Come and join us. No, don't get up, Waldemar. But, my dear chap, what on earth has happened to your hat? The ribbon is all coming off. I wish you'd remember that you have to keep up appearances if you are seen about with me. On account of the legation, you know. British prestige and so on. Do make an effort. And have you heard the latest? The funniest thing you ever heard in your life. The Deputy-Chief of the Air Service found the third secretary from the French legation in his wife's room and loosed off a revolver at him and the shot broke a window in the house opposite and smashed a picture of Mussolini, as it happened to be the Italian consulate. There's going to be the hell of a row.'

'Quite right.'

'You don't seem a bit excited by the news. I shan't tell you my secrets in future.'

'I heard something about it all earlier in the afternoon.'

'You can't have people going about breaking windows, even if they are important public figures. Especially if the windows are extra-territorial ones. I must say all my sympathy is with the outraged husband. Not to mention Mussolini.'

Waldemar said: 'Nevertheless it was an unseemly occurrence. He should have challenged the delinquent to a duel in spite of the heavy penalties that attach to duelling for those convicted of that breach of the civil code.'

'What are the penalties?' Lushington said.

'For killing a man in a duel there is sentence of three years' forced labour. The law is very strictly maintained. Sometimes in very exceptional cases of provocation, as in this instance of which we speak when one party's honour has indeed been tarnished, it might be reduced to half that period. But not often.'

Lushington said: 'In that case, should the situation arise, I shall refuse to run the risk of prison. Everyone at home would be sure to hear of it and no one would ever believe that I had been put there for duelling.'

Da Costa said: 'I hope to goodness Pope does not get himself into trouble of that sort one of these days. I hear that he is a very susceptible man and he is such a snob that it would be bound to be no one less than a Minister's wife.'

'I found Pope reading my letters this morning.'

'The man lives on his nerves. Obviously you have got to

116

put up with something from a man as nervy as that. He's an excellent valet. You expect too much.'

'I don't mind his living on his own nerves. I object to his living on mine.'

Waldemar said: 'This Mr. Pope? I often hear you speak of him. He is by chance a secretary at your legation?'

Da Costa said: 'Well, he's not exactly that; but you can take it from me that without Pope our legation would not keep open for five minutes. It would just cease to exist.'

'Impossible!'

'My dear Waldemar,' Da Costa said, 'it's nothing more than the truth. And now I must leave you because I have a heavy evening before me with the Hedevarys. I believe, by the way, your pretty friend Madame Mavrin is going to be there. Shall I give her your love? And before I go you must congratulate Waldemar. He has been appointed aide-de-camp to General Kuno.'

'You have? Congratulations.'

Waldemar said: 'I thank you both for your congratulations, gentlemen. It is indeed for me a high honour. May I prove myself worthy of it. And only yesterday I was thinking that General Kuno was displeased with me because not long ago he saw me at a late hour with you in a house of amusement. But now I go no more to such places. They are not for those who would make a career.'

Da Costa: 'You're right, Waldemar. They are not. That is one of the reasons why you see me in that sort of place so seldom. I am ambitious.'

He laughed piercingly and, getting up, took his hat and coat and scarf from the chair beside him. He spent some time in dressing up in all his clothes and then, waving his hand, he made his way between the tables and the palms. Lushington and Waldemar sat on in silence. Several business men were arguing gutturally in other corners of the lounge and one had put his feet up on a chair and had gone to sleep. Waldemar blinked and moved his feet about. Then he moistened his lips and said:

'You will take dinner with me, Mr. Lushington? It would be a great pleasure. I invite you.'

Lushington said that he would like very much to take dinner, and Waldemar suggested that they should go first to where he lived so that he could change from top-boots. After that they would dine in the mess of his regiment. He said:

'But first we will go back and you may meet my brothers.'

'How many?'

'They are two.'

As they went along the central boulevard and through the public gardens Waldemar began to speak of his fiancée. She worked in a travel agency and they had not yet enough money to get married, but in two years he would have become a real captain and she would be at the head of her department at the office, so that by then, with their combined incomes, they would have enough to live on. In answer to Lushington's question, Waldemar said he did not mind waiting.

'With such good prospects,' he said, 'we cannot complain at a small delay. You agree that we are very lucky?'

'Very.'

'For few is life so easy.'

The Waldemar brothers lived on the outskirts of the town, so that when they reached the end of the public gardens Waldemar decided to take a tram. He sat very upright when they were inside it with his sword held between his legs so that it did not trip up the conductor. He said:

'But it is unsuitable in a young officer to think of

marriage. Women should not be allowed to interfere with the affairs. You agree?'

'With what affairs?'

'The duty.'

'Of course.'

'And then the life of a soldier is difficult. There is so much gaiety. Last week our Colonel's wife gave an evening festival. All the officers had to be present. Only a fortnight before that the artillery corps organised a dance. Soon there will be preparations for the ball at the House of the Knights. In such an atmosphere of pleasure it is hard to think always of the work that is to be done. And besides, one does not readily give up one's bachelor freedom.'

Waldemar pursed his lips. He became lost in thought. Later he said:

'But I am fortunate. Many young officers in my regiment have debts. One I know owes as much as a whole half-year's pay. At least I have not that to reproach myself with.'

They arrived at the Waldemar flat and went into a narrow hall. In this hall there were three pegs and a uniform cap and overcoat and sword hung on two of them. On the shelf above the pegs were three steel helmets and three revolver holsters. Waldemar put his cap and coat and sword on the third peg. Then he led the way along the passage and opened the door at the end of it. They came into a small room with a table in the middle of it at which two young men in uniform were sitting reading. They wore blue breeches instead of crimson ones like Waldemar. When they saw Lushington they stood up, brought their heels together, and bowed. Waldemar said:

'These are my brothers. This one speaks English, but not well. Always he studies it, but he is not yet proficient. He can read, but he cannot speak well. The other one is not clever. He can speak only his own language and German. He is backward. A slow boy.'

Lushington shook hands. He shook hands with the slow boy first, for humanitarian reasons. Everyone stood more or less at attention facing everybody else. It was like an amateur two-minutes' silence. At the end of it Lushington said:

'I see that they are not in the same regiment as yourself.'

'This one is in the Corps of Engineers. He that is backward in the 8th Regiment of the Line.'

'Very nice.'

After a while everyone sat down. The brothers were young men on the same lines as Waldemar, but both of them were larger in build and had redder faces. They said that they had just come back from barracks and, as for some reason neither of them were dining in mess that night, they had been putting in some serious reading before going out to the evening meal. Waldemar said:

'See, this brother reads an English book.'

He took the English book from the brother who was reading it and gave it to Lushington for his inspection. Lushington looked at the title. It was *The Ordeal of Richard Feverel*. Waldemar said: 'And now you will excuse? I go to take off my breeches.'

Lushington handed back the book to the English-speaking brother. He said:

'A bit of an ordeal for you too, I expect?'

'Please?'

'I say it must have been a bit of an ordeal for you too—to plough through all that?'

'To plough?'

'To get through it.'

'Please?'

'I mean it's not at all an easy book to read, that's all. It's the kind of book that an Englishman might find it difficult to finish. It's a bit diffuse. Not easy to follow. Some of the ideas are rather out of date and all that.'

'So?'

'I never got to the end of it myself. Somehow I seemed to lose interest. I don't quite know why, because it's a good book in its way. Mental laziness, I suppose.'

'So?'

Waldemar, who had appeared again in the room with some crimson overall trousers which he was engaged in fitting over and buttoning under the soles of his wellingtons, preparatory to putting on both at once, made a shot at possible puritanical motives that might cause Englishmen to fight shy of Meredith and said:

'It is a shocking story, yes?'

'No, no. Not at all. All I say is that some people, myself for example, find it rather an ordeal to get through. Ordeal is too strong a word. I only used it because it was one of the words in the title of the book. I was not speaking seriously.'

'You joke?'

'Yes. I joke.'

Waldemar said: 'It is that which I like so much in you Englishmen. The jokes you have. Always it is the jokes. It is very nice.'

He explained matters to the English-speaking brother and then to the dull one who spoke only two languages. He said to the English-speaking brother:

'It is plain that you do not yet understand the English tongue. Be not so slow. Apply your mind to the study of that most useful language.'

When Waldemar had managed at last to get into his wellingtons he and Lushington left the two brothers, after

I

shaking hands again all round, and walked to the barracks, which were only a few streets away. They had dinner in the mess, a long low room with two tables running down it at which rows of stolid uhlans were seated. Waldemar said:

'I will present to you but the Colonel and the Adjutant. The rest who speak only German would anger you. Later I wish to consult your opinion on the subject of marriage and the relative position of the husband and the wife. I wish to hear your view on so serious a topic. I am glad that we have the night before us so that each can put forward the convictions he may hold on the much discussed perplexities of the married state.'

24

ULTIMATELY it was Da Costa who decided that it would be a good thing to go inland for a week-end's skiing. He had said that Lushington must certainly ski at some time before he went back to England and that he himself wished to do something of the sort in the near future because he considered that this might send up his shares with Bellamy, who approved of outdoor sports. Lushington, whose mind was seldom free from ruminations as to subjects for newspaper articles, was easily persuaded. Cortney agreed to go with them. In the end all the arrangements for the journey were left in Cortney's hands and were carried out by him with moderate success. They arrived at the place with all their luggage and, although at one stage of the journey Lushington mislaid one of the skis he had hired, this was found later in the dining-car.

This part of the country was more hilly than the land along the coast. There were unending downs covered in snow and clumps of pine trees that stood beside frozen water. In the middle of the day the sun was bright and threw up a dazzling glare from the white slopes and the stretches of ice. Later the wind would get up as the sun began to lose its strength and the surface snow would be blown like dust across the tracks of the skis. There were no houses. As far as the horizon there seemed to be not even a peasant's hut. Below was the hotel and the station with the few outbuildings that belonged to them. The railway line ran as far as a signal-box and then that too seemed to disappear in the snow. At certain seasons the hotel was full of people, but this was the wrong time of year.

All that day they had been out on skis and now they were returning to the hotel. They came down the last incline at full speed and both Da Costa and Lushington fell where the ground rose slightly and then slanted away again suddenly. Cortney at the end of the descent did a christiania and, turning, watched them get up. Da Costa with his long eccentric face and darkened spectacles was the English milord of almost any French dramatic production. This effect was heightened by his hat, bought in the Tyrol, and the short square mackintosh coat with big buttons on it that covered the upper half of his body. Da Costa picked up his Tyrolese hat and began to brush the snow off it. Lushington rose from the ground and said, not for the first time that day:

'Why on earth aren't one's feet fixed into these skis as they are in the Swiss ones?'

'It is the custom in this part of Europe. It is easier when you are used to it. You can see whole battalions of troops going through evolutions on these skis. It's a wonderful sight.'

'I can believe you.'

'All dressed in white for camouflage.'

'Touching it must be.'

Cortney was some way ahead of them now. He moved easily on his skis and sometimes burst into snatches of song that lasted for several minutes. His medium was a hollow baritone. If the words were at all familiar Da Costa would join in with a stentorian and toneless lament, like some dreadful manifestation of African grief. These cacophonies echoed across the foot-hills and the wastes of snow and pine trees. At the end of them Da Costa would roar with laughter and try to yodel. The snow was beginning to descend again now in small flakes that blew sharply across their faces and into their eyes. The dusk, the tragic northern shadows of late afternoon, had begun to fall. The sun was already making bright stains on the snow between the stems of the pine trees and across the ice of the lake. Da Costa said:

'We must press on. We want to get back to the hotel before dark. If one is too late there is often no food left.'

'Do you make a habit of spending your week-ends here?'

'Why are you so bad-tempered? What has happened? Has it come off again?'

'The strap has broken.'

'Can't you fix it so that it lasts as far as the hotel?'

'No.'

'Curtis! Curtis! Cur-tis! Have you got some string? Some stri-ing?'

But Cortney was far away and he could not hear them because he was singing. The throaty words were carried back on the wind and past them:

> '. . . *Oh my name is Samuel Hall.* . . .
> *Samuel Hall.* . . .
> *And I hate you one and all.* . . .
> *You're a bunch of* . . .'

'It's no good, I'm afraid.'

'No, I'll carry them.'

'It isn't far.'

'Oh, no.'

By the time they had come to the hotel the snow was falling heavily. The hotel was a wooden chalet-like structure standing on a slight eminence and dominating the only other building, the railway station which gave the place its name and which was made for the most part of corrugated iron and barbed wire. As they passed the platform they saw waiting there for the train, due in a few hours time for the capital, a peasant family. Steaming, the peasants stood about or sat on their wooden boxes, so encased in clothes that it was difficult to tell which were women and which men. One of the smaller children raised its arm in surprise as Da Costa passed, but the others were impassive, too far from reality or too near to it to know or care whether this was a human being like themselves who looked so strange. Cortney, who had waited for the other two, had taken off his skis and was carrying them over his shoulder. He nodded in the direction of the peasants and said:

'See them. The children of the soil. The patient toilers now the day is done. Don't they make you think——'

Lushington and Da Costa walked towards the yard and stacked their skis in the shed. Then they went into the hotel, which was almost empty at this time of year. It was very warm inside but none of the doors fitted, so that any sounds that were made reverberated along the wooden corridors. They ordered supper at once and went up to change from their ski-ing clothes. It was sometimes possible to obtain water to wash in before the evening meal.

When he came downstairs again Lushington was surprised to find Cortney in front of the fire talking to Count Scherbatcheff. The Count was wearing his overcoat, although the room was stifling, and he explained that he had come up to this part of the country for a few days for the sake of his health. Here the ground was higher and the air was better and the doctor had suggested that a week's ski-ing might do him good.

'My health has been bad,' he said, 'and my relations do not understand me. But I am glad that all of you are here.

In the evenings we can talk as we are doing now and it will be less dull than when I was here alone.'

The others had their meal, but Count Scherbatcheff refused to eat because he said that he did not feel well. He sat there in his overcoat and drank a little beer and joined in the conversation. The food in the hotel was plain, but not bad, although there was a chronic danger that owing to the difficulties of transport there might be nothing to eat at all. This eventuality was harped on by Da Costa, who used it as a sort of weapon with which to bully the others and the proprietor of the hotel himself. That evening, however, there was plenty to eat and after dinner they pushed back the table and sat in the dining-room in front of the fire. In answer to a remark made by Da Costa, Cortney said:

'Cute? I'll say they are cute. Why, there isn't a town from Maine to California that can't produce a year's debs to rival those of any other city in any other country that you may like to name.'

Count Scherbatcheff said: 'There are times when women seem to me no more than the illusions that the camera throws on the shaking screen. The shadow of life. In the mythology of the Scandinavians they tell of creatures who present to the eye the appearance of flesh and blood and beauty. And yet, going behind them, they are discovered to be flat. They have no substance. They are like pictures hung on an easel that have no thickness.'

'Why, Count, you wouldn't say that if I took you around. And one of these days I will. We three and the Count will throw a wild party. And we'll throw it somewhere the right side of Mason-Dixon. You won't think the girls are illusions there. I'll see to that.'

Da Costa said: 'Personally I absolutely agree with Scherbatcheff. I would rather not. But I do. I should like to have a temperament like that new Spanish secretary. I never saw anything like the success he was having at the Arnhfeldts' the other night.'

Cortney said: 'You've said it. All the pretty women in the place at his heels. Madame Mavrin, Countess Arnhfeldt, Mrs. Mitsu, the whole lot of them.'

Lushington said: 'Countess Arnhfeldt certainly. But I don't know why you mention Madame Mavrin. I didn't notice that she seemed particularly keen on him.'

'You know, Lushington, those dagos have a way with them. We just can't compete. It's one of the things I have had to learn and which you will have to learn too.'

'But just because Madame Mavrin may have danced with him a couple of times I see no reason why you should spread scandals about her.'

'Scandal? Why, I should say I wouldn't spread scandals about her, Lushington. Why, there isn't a lady in the whole town whom I hold in greater respect than Frau Mavrin. I should say not. All I said was that she and a good many more of them seemed to like the looks of that young Spaniard more than I did myself.'

'Well, that's just what I said.'

'What are you disagreeing with me for, then?'

'I mean that I said that that was what you said before and now you are denying it. I didn't say anything of the sort myself. I don't think it.'

'Don't think what?'

'That Madame Mavrin was getting off with that Spaniard.'

'Neither do I. All I said was that she seemed to like him.'

'You didn't. You inferred that she liked him in a way that she should not do. It's a perfect disgrace. It's fellows like you who start these stories and then trouble follows.'

'But see here, Lushington——'

Count Scherbatcheff said: 'Mr. Lushington is quite right,

Mr. Cortney. You spoke no doubt unintentionally but at the same time most improperly of Madame Mavrin. Men have had to fight duels for less. I do not blame you because I feel sure that you were not thinking about what you were saying, but at the same time I should counsel that you speak with greater prudence in future.'

Da Costa said: 'I can't imagine what has come over you and Scherbatcheff, unless you have eaten too much and he has eaten too little. Cortney never said a word against Madame Mavrin. Anyway I expect the Spaniard preferred Countess Arnhfeldt. In my opinion there is no doubt at all that she is the better-looking of the two.'

Lushington said: 'To say that is merely silly. In the first place she does not look nearly so interesting. Anyway the Spaniard obviously did not think that Countess Arnhfeldt was the more attractive. That was clear from his behaviour.'

'But I thought you said that he only danced with Madame Mavrin twice all the evening?'

'What I said was that neither of them had behaved in a way to provoke the scandal which I thought Cortney was spreading. However, as I see that you are bent on circulating a tissue of inventions yourself, I will say no more and you can broadcast what you like.'

'But see here, Lushington—and you, Count—you must understand that I never meant a word against Madame Mavrin. I can't see how you can have thought that I did. And Da Costa is quite right. It was Countess Arnhfeldt that he had his eye on and I don't blame him. Much as I admire Madame Mavrin I hold the Countess the greater beauty of the two.'

'Well, if you think that, nothing surprises me.'

Count Scherbatcheff, who was having a bad fit of coughing at that moment, moved his head from side to side to show that he too found these words incredible, but he was unable to speak the protests that he evidently wanted to make. Da Costa said:

'Come on, let's play bridge. I have some cards here. I can't imagine how all this started. Or why.'

25

EVERYONE felt better after the week-end spent ski-ing, except Count Scherbatcheff, who felt worse. The Count decided that to be left alone in the hotel after the others were gone would depress him too much and so he travelled back with them, sleeping on the floor of the wagon-lit shared by Lushington and Cortney. The journey was not long, but the best train went after midnight and Da Costa insisted that they must have sleepers. In the morning Cortney forgot that Count Scherbatcheff was on the floor and put his bare foot on the Count's face when he got out of his bunk, but Count Scherbatcheff took this in very good part and said that much worse things had happened to him during the Revolution. Da Costa shared a compartment with a priest who wore a square Assyrian beard. They kept the rest of the train awake all night by arguing about religion in bad French. Both of them looked very pale and bad-tempered the next morning and the priest got up early and stood for the rest of the journey in the corridor and ate something which he had brought with him in a paper bag. When they arrived at the capital Count Scherbatcheff refused all offers of a lift and he was last seen hurrying away, carrying his wicker suitcase, which was the size and shape of a coffin and had several straps round it. The others went to their respective homes and all of them met again that evening at a party given by Madame Bitulescu.

26

LUSHINGTON, who had been spending the previous two or three days writing up accounts of the ski-ing expedition for various periodicals, was standing in front of the looking-glass in his sitting-room, tying his white tie, and because when someone knocked at the door he thought that the Bellamys might have arrived unexpectedly early, he slipped on his dressing-gown before opening it. It was not the Bellamys, however. It was Ortrud. She said:

'I came straight up. You do not mind?'

'Of course not. But I shall have to go out in a minute. The Bellamys are picking up Cortney and me in the legation car as we are all going to the same place for dinner.'

'You are going out tonight?'

'I have to.'

'But I am free tonight and we can go out together. You must put them off. You can leave a message at the hotel desk to say that you are ill.'

'No, I can't possibly. Besides, they may be here at any moment. I told them to come here for a cocktail before we went on.'

'But surely you can put them off? We have not met for so long. You go away to the country and leave me. Would you not prefer to have dinner with me? But perhaps you would not?'

'You know I should. How silly you are. But surely you understand that I cannot do so at this moment. It must be obvious.'

'Not at all. If you were really fond of me you would have suggested it yourself. But I understand. You would rather go out with the Bellamys. Naturally I see that they are more important people than I am.'

'Really, please. Do not be so ridiculous. What has happened to you? This is most unlike you.'

'It is unlike me to want to see you? Do you think that is true? I can remember the time when you wanted to see me.'

'But you know that I want to see you now. I would much rather go out with you than with the Bellamys. But I can't put them off when they may arrive in my room at any moment.'

'No, no. I understand.'

'But how can I?'

'No, of course not. Naturally not.'

'Ortrud?'

'Good-bye, then.'

'Please?'

'Perhaps we may meet again some time before you leave.'

'When you are in a less ridiculous mood, I hope.'

'And you less rude.'

She slammed the door a little. Lushington went on with his dressing. Pope, who for some reason had put out his dinner-jacket to wear that night, had also hidden his white waistcoat, but Lushington found it at last in a box on the top of the wardrobe. This was reached by putting a suitcase on a chair, and then stepping on to it from the table. As he was climbing down, precariously, from this edifice there was another knock on the sitting-room door.

'Come in.'

It was Da Costa this time, who said:

'I was passing and saw a light in your sitting-room so I thought I'd look in. You don't mind my coming straight up, I hope.'

'Have a cigarette. Take your goloshes off. The Bellamys are coming at any moment. They are giving me a lift in the Rolls and are having a cocktail here first.'

'In that case I don't think I'll stop.'

'Why not?'

'It's not that I dislike Bellamy. On the contrary. I think that in many ways he's a very good fellow. And I like Mrs. Bellamy as well. On occasions she can be charming. But since if I stay I shall inevitably be drawn into talking shop I shall instead go to my own home and read a little before dinner.'

'All right. Then we shall meet to-morrow at the Koskis'?'

Da Costa nodded. He lit a cigarette and went away. Lushington examined the white waistcoat. It had several black marks across the front. He understood now why Pope had put out his dinner-jacket to wear that night. It would now be necessary to find another waistcoat. He went into the bedroom and began to go through the drawers. There were no white waistcoats. Then he pulled a box from under the bed and began to throw its contents on the floor. He was lucky, and in a few minutes found a garment that was not too crumpled to wear. While he was putting the buttons in, the telephone bell rang.

'Hullo?'

It was Flosshilde from the desk in the hotel lounge. She said in her slow English:

'A gentleman to see you. And two ladies.'

'Ask them to come up.'

Lushington fumbled with the last button of the waistcoat. He wondered who the other lady was. He said:

'It is Mr. Bellamy, of course, of the British legation?'

'Please?'

'It is Mr. and Mrs. Bellamy? The English *chargé*

d'affaires? The gentleman who often walks about without an overcoat?'

'The gentleman said that his name was Count Bobel. He did not tell me the names of the ladies.'

'Count Bobel! Tell them to wait for a moment. Tell them that I am engaged and can see no one for the time being.'

'For the time being? Please I do not understand.'

'Now! Now! Stop them!'

'They have started on their way up.'

'Prevent them quickly.'

'They have already ascended in the lift.'

The knock came at the sitting-room door at the exact moment at which Lushington was turning the handle to get out into the passage and send down his visitors in the lift from which they had emerged. The door opened inwards and Count Bobel entered holding out his hand and beaming. He was followed by two women. Count Bobel said:

'Mr. Lushington, *mon cher,* how splendid to see you again.'

To gain time Lushington took the hand and shook it. Count Bobel said:

'Mr. Lushington, I was about to make a little trip into the country with these two ladies. There is a small hotel along the coast that we could reach in time for dinner. Outside I have a sleigh. It occurred to me that with a fourth there would be more pleasure for all concerned. Will you not therefore join us? In that way we shall be *une partie carrée.*'

Glancing at the girls, Lushington saw that they were the ones who had sat near his table the night he had gone to Maxim's with Da Costa, Waldemar and Cortney. The one who had worn riding costume on that occasion was evidently dressed at this moment in something of the sort under her coat, because she wore top-boots and a three-cornered hat that spoke of stag hunts in Normandy and the meet on St. Hubert's day. The other, the blonde, was so encased in furs that he could barely see her face at all, but the features that were visible showed that she still looked cross. The faces of both ladies were made up for the savage glare of night-club illuminations. Lushington, remembering that he was in his shirt sleeves, took up his tail-coat and began to struggle into it. Count Bobel was looking round the room with interest. He said:

'This lady speaks English.'

Outside, the clock above the National Theatre struck the half-hour. Lushington remembered that Da Costa had once reported an observation made by Bellamy to the effect that unpunctuality in a diplomatist spelled ruin. The Bellamys would therefore arrive at the hotel at any moment now. It would be necessary to take action. Count Bobel said:

'I will introduce. This is the Marquise Clothilde de Madragore. And this is the Princess Varvara.'

Lushington shook hands. The Marquise said:

'Yes, please. Speak English, mister.'

Count Bobel, who had sat down on the sofa and was lighting one of his amber cigarettes, said:

'You understand that it is not so much English that she speaks and thus it will not matter if I mention in front of her a little matter which I do not wish to forget. The young girl at the desk downstairs. She has been here long?'

'I don't know at all.'

'You have noticed her?'

'I have seen her, of course. What do you mean? I do not understand you.'

'You would not mind if I were to ask her out?'

'Why in the world should I?'

136

'You have not approached her, no?'

'Only for my letters.'

Count Bobel threw up his hands. He said:

'Ah, your English stiffness! When shall I become accustomed to it? But I must tell you how I met the young lady who is at the desk downstairs. It was at a little cabaret on the river bank. She was with an Englishman, a good fellow, a Mr. Pope who said he knew you. He is perhaps a secretary at your legation, yes?'

'No.'

'Never mind, then. Later I won a little money from him doing tricks with matches. The young lady was with him. I am not a vain man but I could not help seeing that she had taken a fancy to me.'

'Indeed?'

The smell from Count Bobel's cigarette was filling the room. Certainly the moment to act was approaching. The Princess Varvara had begun to repair her face and patchouli was added to the scent of amber. The Marquise produced a lipstick from her vanity bag. Lushington took Count Bobel by the lapel of his coat and led him into the corner of the room.

'Count Bobel, I must speak to you plainly. It was a misunderstanding that they showed you up here. I am busy. I must inform you that the door opposite leads to my bedroom.'

'Ah-ha?'

'You are disturbing me. I cannot come on this trip. I am not alone. I am occupied. This is an important moment in my life.'

'You mean, Mr. Lushington——'

'Exactly.'

'Une femme——?'

'Must I put it more bluntly?'

'But——'

'Have I said enough?'

Count Bobel fell into an arm-chair and began to roar with falsetto laughter. He said:

'You English! You English! When shall I become accustomed to your way? But why did you not say so at once? And I myself was so slow that I thought you were putting your clothes on. Never for one moment did I guess that you were taking them off. You are cunning, *mon cher*.'

Still laughing he began to explain the situation to the ladies in a language that was unfamiliar to Lushington. They agreed with the Count that it was a good joke. Even the blonde relaxed a little. They were still enjoying it when the telephone bell rang. Lushington took up the receiver.

'Hullo?'

'Mr. and Mrs. Bellamy,' Flosshilde said.

'Will you ask them to wait for one moment?'

'They said that you expected them and that they would make their way up.'

Lushington snapped down the receiver. He took Count Bobel by the arm.

'And now, Count Bobel——'

The Count could hardly speak, he was laughing so much; but he managed to get up and to say:

'One moment, Mr. Lushington. I have here some post-cards which I had intended to show you. I feel certain that they will amuse you. They are free, but for that reason they are none the less funny. I brought them specially with me tonight that you might see them because I forgot to show them to you on the voyage. They are here. One moment——'

'Count Bobel, some other time. I must insist.'

'But look just at this one.'

'Not now!'

Lushington put him through the door and the Marquise and the Princess after him. As he shut the door behind him he heard the clang of the lift as it arrived at his landing. He had time hardly to stamp out the cigarette that Count Bobel in his amusement had left lying on the edge of the table and to throw the stub of it into the waste-paper basket when he found that the Bellamys had arrived.

Later in the evening Mrs. Bellamy said:

'Of course, some people prefer the Bristol to this hotel. It may not be so comfortable, but it is certainly quieter. You see some very impossible people in here at times.'

'I have noticed some odd people in the lounge on occasions.'

Mrs. Bellamy said: 'We passed three very extraordinary people in the corridor just outside this room when we arrived. A man and two women. Did you notice them, Trevor?'

'Well, I hope they won't any of them decide to come in here,' Lushington said. 'As a matter of fact I had thought of moving to the Bristol. It would be, as you say, quieter. But then I shan't be staying here so very much longer.'

27

AND then one day Count Scherbatcheff died. For a long'
time he had looked more and more ill and the troubles
with his stomach had become increasingly serious. He
could be seen in the streets, hunched up and wearing his
astrakhan cap, as he hurried along, returning from a visit
to some other member of the Russian colony. This was
his occupation, although he also sat sometimes in bars or
sipped tea in the lounge of the hotel. He never appeared
at diplomatic gatherings and all his friends were Russian.
His grandmother sent Lushington an invitation to the
funeral, which took place in the Orthodox cathedral. Ortrud
sent a wreath but did not attend the ceremony because of
what her husband felt about Russians. After the service
they followed the coffin to a cemetery in a distant part of
the town, farther even than the Scherbatcheff flat, and they
passed by the stacks of empty petrol tins and the big shells
of uncompleted buildings with cranes on top of them. Da
Costa and Cortney came too and wore top-hats. Pope
offered to lend Lushington a top-hat for the funeral, but, as
the weather was cold, Lushington said that he would prefer
to wear his own fur cap. He walked in the procession next
to Count Scherbatcheff's uncle, the man with the shaved
head who wore a grey military overcoat and the cross of
St. George. On the way home Lushington saw him put
his hand in the pocket of the overcoat and take out some
cigarettes which he evidently carried loose there, instead of
in a case. Count Scherbatcheff's grandmother walked in the

procession too and wept into a small lace handkerchief.

Later that week there were political disturbances and someone hit someone else in the House of Deputies. There was also a riot at one of the timber yards up the river and the mounted gendarmes were called out. Some people said that there was going to be a revolution, but this was considered to be unlikely because General Kuno was known to have such matters well in hand, and more often the topic of conversation was the ball at the House of the Knights which was to take place soon and which it was intended to make more of a success than ever before, although Baroness Puckler had pointed out that, whatever they did, nothing could rival what these entertainments had been like when she was a girl. Sometimes it occurred to Lushington that soon he would be going back to England. He found that he talked less to Da Costa about Lucy. In fact on several occasions Da Costa himself had brought her into their conversations. He often saw Ortrud.

28

COMING down the stairs of the hotel into the lounge, Lushington was surprised to see Professor Mavrin standing at the desk talking to Flosshilde. Lushington touched him on the arm and said good-morning. The Professor turned and said:

'Mr. Lushington, I am so delighted to find you at home. I am free this afternoon. I have no lectures. I hoped that perhaps you would accompany me on a walk.'

'I should like nothing better.'

Flosshilde said: 'Herr Lushington, here are three letters and a postcard for you. There is additional tax to pay on them. They have not enough stamps.'

Lushington glanced at the letters. All were from Lucy. He paid Flosshilde, put the letters in his pocket, and said to the Professor:

'That is the sort of thing that women never remember. To put enough stamps on a letter going abroad.'

The Professor laughed and stroked his tattered moustache, which gave him something of the air of a sea-lion. He said:

'They are from your fiancée perhaps and therefore you do not mind?'

'Well, no. Not exactly. Just a friend, you know.'

They went out into the streets and walked down the steps that led to the river. It was a sunny afternoon with a sharp wind blowing inland from the islands. The Professor said:

'It is interesting to me what you said, that your letters came from a woman who was a friend. That is something that only England enjoys. The friendship between the sexes when the more deep relationship remains in the background. With all our advances in the sphere of modern thought we have not yet achieved such in this country. And you yourself, Mr. Lushington, do you never feel that a friendship of this sort may not become disturbing?'

'Of course one hears of instances where it may be said to have done so.'

'In this country it would seem impossible that such frankness can exist. The women themselves are not yet prepared for it. The men, too, hardly wish for it. And this brings me to a subject which I would discuss with you because I believe you to be a man of understanding. I wish to speak to you about my wife.'

Lushington assumed an expression of interest. He wondered whether the Professor was anything of a shot and if combatants were allowed to wear glasses in a duel. The snow in the early morning would be very dazzling to the eyes. Swords were clearly out of the question. The Professor continued:

'For some time I have noticed that she has not been herself. She is absent-minded. She weeps easily. Sometimes she is unnecessarily high-spirited. At other times she is sunk into deep despondency. Have you remarked these things? Indeed you cannot fail to have remarked them.'

'I thought that perhaps her temperament made her act as you describe. I have, of course, noticed that she has moods. But then I have known her for comparatively so short a time.'

'What do you think such behaviour signifies?'

'I cannot imagine.'

'But is it not only too clear?'

'Not to me, Professor.'

'Come, come, Mr. Lushington,' said the Professor, almost testily, 'you are a journalist. A man of the world. When do women behave in such a way? Is it not when they are in love?'

'Yes, I suppose it is, now that I come to think of it.'

'Of course it is. And I will tell you. I think that such is the case with my wife.'

'But that is quite right surely? That she should be in love?'

'You misunderstand me. I cannot flatter myself that I am the cause of these manifestations. On the contrary.'

'No?'

'No,' said the Professor. 'And what is more than that, I believe that I know the man whom she loves.'

'Really?'

They were crossing the Nikolai Bridge now. An apprehension was raised in Lushington's mind that the Professor might have hired a gang to throw him into the river from this point. Single-handed, he supposed, he could tackle the Professor himself, who could not be strong after the hardships he had undergone during the Revolution. When they were half-way across the Professor stopped, and for several minutes pointed out places of interest in the town which could be seen best from the bridge. Several suspicious-looking characters passed while he was doing this, but the farther bank was reached without incident. The Professor said:

'But to return to the problem of domestic life: I will not ask you to guess who it is that I have in my mind, but I feel sure that you would guess correctly.'

'Oh but, on the contrary, I feel sure that I should not.'

'No, Mr. Lushington, you do not give your imagination due justice. But we leave that for the moment. For it is of the theory of the matter that I would speak to you and not of personalities. I wish to know from you how in England the situation would be considered.'

'Well, of course, situations of that kind have, to a great degree, to be judged on their own merits.'

'You think that?'

'Most certainly.'

'And such is the accepted English view?'

'It is and it isn't.'

'Exactly,' said the Professor. 'That is precisely what I myself feel. Sometimes I think this. Sometimes that. We must, for example, recognise that the economic position of women has altered in the last few years in a way which it is impossible to estimate. Woman has become her own master.'

'And very often someone else's mistress.'

'Very good!' said the Professor. 'Very good! Excellent! I must remember that and write it down. Will you repeat it once more? The modern woman is not only becoming her own master, she has already become another's mistress. I shall say that when I have to attend the dinner of the senior professors which takes place next week. It is a most true and profound saying. It will entertain them greatly and no doubt add in some measure to my popularity. But to return to a more serious view of the question, do you hold with me that women should be allowed considerable liberty?'

'Naturally I agree with you.'

'I am glad that you agree on that point. Yet this liberty must not be allowed to develop into licence. You agree there too? Not licence.'

'Oh, most certainly not.'

'But who is to tell where liberty may end and licence begin?'

'That must surely remain a question for each individual to settle for him or for herself?'

'But is it not possible in the case of a husband and a wife that what may appear a necessary relaxation to the one, bears to the other all the marks of unjustifiable conduct?'

'Do you think so?'

'It would appear most apparent.'

'I had not thought of that. Perhaps you are right.'

'And yet I do not wish, Mr. Lushington, that for one moment you should think that I am out of touch with the ideas of the present day. On the contrary I have myself always been a steadfast upholder of advanced thought. But it is impossible to disregard the intricacies, the compromises, which must accompany any reconciliation of the teachings of the doctrinaire who may content himself with hypothetical cases of comparative simplicity, with the more complicated and personal problems of the individual world in which we live. You yourself will surely be with me in admitting the considerable range of obstacles which are on the road to a better understanding?'

'I quite agree with you there. I think that you are quite right.'

'Very well then. We may proceed. But first you will not mind my telling you why I choose you for these confidences. It is this. I have noticed that my wife speaks always of you and to you, Mr. Lushington, with considerable asperity. I feel sure that she likes you, but I cannot blind myself to the fact that there is at the same time something about you that affects adversely her nerves. You do not, I hope, mind my telling you these things? You do not mind, Mr. Lushington?'

'Not in the least.'

'I am glad. It is for this reason that I said those words. You know my wife and yet, because she is always so brusque with you, she cannot fail to have caused you annoyance and therefore there is less breach of confidence on your part if you tell me what you think of her. You comprehend my meaning?'

'But——'

'One moment, please. I believe that the reason of her attitude towards you is this. You are a friend of Mr. Da Costa. It appears to me that she is *jealous* of your friendship with Mr. Da Costa. I do not think that she herself even is aware of this. It is all in the realm of the subconscious. I do not know indeed whether she is even aware of her own feelings for Mr. Da Costa, but I am confident that it is towards him that she feels a strong attachment.'

'Da Costa!'

'You are surprised. You cannot accustom yourself to the idea of a married woman feeling drawn towards a man who is not her husband. That is in many ways the right point of view for you to take. I admire it, but I cannot say that I share it. My reading and my experience have taught me otherwise. But having told you so much you will not perhaps mind my asking you a question about your friend? Do you think, Mr. Lushington, that the feelings of which I speak are in any way reciprocated by him?'

'I feel sure that they are not. There is nothing of which I feel more certain. You can set your mind at rest on that point.'

'You can really assure me?'

'I am confident of it.'

The Professor said: 'In that case I feel greatly relieved. Because although I am a student of advanced thought I cannot conceal from myself that I still retain many unprogressive prejudices.'

'But even were anything so unlikely, so distasteful, the case as that my friend Da Costa and your wife possessed the feelings for each other that you suggest, I cannot see why my friendship for him should make your wife jealous?'

'My dear Mr. Lushington, you do not understand. In the realm of the sub-conscious there are dark and secret places, strange emotions that do not distinguish, as does our waking consciousness, between such kindred feelings as love and friendship. These have power over the actions of the individual of which he himself or she herself is wholly unaware. I tell you this from the depths of my experience.'

'But, my dear Professor, I cannot allow the implications of what you have said to pass without protest. I feel justified in objecting most strongly to your suggestion that your wife is jealous of me on account of my friendship.'

'My dear Mr. Lushington, jealousy is far too definite a word. I used it only to indicate the general tendency of her attitude to give support to what I had already told you about her. Perhaps I expressed what I mean in a way that was not good. You must remember that I have but a limited knowledge of your language.'

'No, you are wrong. You speak English excellently. I am astonished at the degree of excellence with which everyone in this country speaks English.'

'You are too kind. But you understand that we must learn the language of the larger countries. It is necessary. As I was——'

'At the same time, Professor, I feel a little vexed that you should have made the remarks which you did. I think I am right.'

'My dear Mr. Lushington, I cannot imagine why you should think that. That indeed was the very last impression that I should like to give. Why, often people have asked me if I am not jealous of Baroness Puckler. In jest, naturally. And that was the spirit in which I took their remarks. Nevertheless, if you understand me——'

'Exactly, Professor. You have said enough. But do not let us discuss the matter further. I would rather not.'

'Perhaps you are right, Mr. Lushington. Perhaps I was going too far in what I said. Although I must assure you that I intended to convey nothing of what I fear may have been in your mind. I can only apologise——'

'No, no. Please do not apologise. We have said enough about the matter. Let us talk of something more pleasant. On such a lovely day as this, is it not a pity to discuss psychology? A little morbid, do not you think?'

'You are indeed right, Mr. Lushington, and again——'

'Please, my dear Professor, please say no more about it.'

They walked on for some time in silence. The wind was blowing the powdered snow off the parapets of the river's embankment. There was a fresh scent in the air of wood smoke. Lushington said:

'You have always promised to take me to the National Museum. Shall we go there now as we are about to pass it?'

'An excellent idea. Excellent. And besides, the wind is becoming cold.'

29

THEY went up the steps of the museum and worked systematically· through the halls of national costume, folk lore, pottery, agriculture, industries, and fossils. In this last room they found Da Costa. He was leaning heavily on one of the glass cases, which creaked under his weight so that at any moment it seemed possible that he might fall through it. He looked up when Lushington and the Professor entered and laughed so· loudly that an attendant hurried in from the next room to see what had happened. Da Costa said:

'Fancy meeting here! How are you, Herr Professor? And how is Frau Mavrin? It is quite a long time since I have seen you both.'

Lushington said: 'Professor Mavrin and I have been for a walk and as he has always promised to show me round here I thought it would be a good opportunity as we were passing. But I didn't know you were in the habit of coming here.'

'I'm not,' Da Costa said. 'To tell the truth, I have hardly ever been here before. But since Scherbatcheff's funeral I have become interested in death. I can't tell you why exactly, but there it is. It occurred to me that this would be a good place to consider it in.'

He laughed again and the whole of his face worked up and down. The Professor said:

'You are too young a man to think about death, Mr. Da Costa. You should think about life, love, your career.

Death you should leave to old gentlemen like myself.'

Da Costa said: 'I think about those things too sometimes. But on the whole I find thinking about death a better mental exercise. For one thing, one knows less about it than the other three.'

Lushington said: 'I was very sorry about Scherbatcheff myself. I don't think you knew him, did you, Professor? He was a Russian who travelled out here with me on the same boat.'

The Professor said: 'As a Russian I should not have known him. I know no Russians. But for your sake I am sorry that he is dead.'

Da Costa said: 'He was a nice man and, whatever people may say about it, one does not want to die. Anyway not just yet. At least that is the conclusion that I have just come to.'

The Professor said: 'You are right, Mr. Da Costa. The instinct of self-preservation remains with us in spite of all melancholies and discomforts. Only yesterday I was speaking to General Kuno, who, as you must know, has many times been threatened with death, about this very subject.'

Da Costa said: 'Well, fortunately, no one dislikes me enough yet actually to assassinate me, although I must say I caught Bellamy looking at me in a very funny way the other day. Perhaps he will bribe Pope to poison me.'

Lushington said: 'I suppose they will get General Kuno in the end?'

Da Costa said: 'Nonsense. People like that bear charmed lives. Tons of dynamite get thrown at them every year and only the public standing round get damaged.'

The Professor said: 'I repeat, Mr. Da Costa, that you should not think of such things. You are too young. You have much time yet. Rather let us examine these fine specimens of the rare chromate of lead which come from

Siberia and this meteorite which fell near this very town in the middle years of the last century. After that you will perhaps permit me to invite you to tea, for I feel sure that my wife will be delighted to see both of you.'

Da Costa said: 'That is very kind of you, Professor. I have some things I particularly want to talk over with Frau Mavrin.'

30

THE façade of the House of the Knights was ornamented
with wooden carvings and gargoyles. Inside, it had not been
redecorated for many years and it was a pleasing mixture of
tastes. 'The ballroom was large and long, not unlike a drill-
hall, and along two sides of it were alcoves in each of which
a figure in armour had been placed. Most of the suits were
seventeenth century in style. A few had casques with long
tails and projecting visors and one or two, of Russian or
Polish origin, curved up to points like Persian helmets. On
the capitals of each of the pillars of the hall the arms of a
noble family had been carved and painted and gilded. These
also were late in date and some of the coats florid in design.
At one end of the room the band from the Café Weber
was playing Strauss and at the other the President sat, a
small man wearing too short evening trousers. He had
been given a high Spanish chair so that his feet were just off
the ground, but he sat there looking happy and interested in
everything that was taking place. A group of cavalrymen
stood behind him, leaning romantically on their sabres,
mopping and mowing at their friends in other parts of the
hall and assisting the room's chiaroscuro with a solid background of red breeches. Everyone of any importance
seemed to be present, although Ortrud had not yet arrived.
Lushington was standing next to the British military attaché,
who had manoeuvred himself behind a high-backed chair,
under cover of which he was undoing the top button of his
trousers, which were, he explained, the ones he had bought

at the time when he had first joined his regiment. Lushington, who had been extending his sympathy, said:

'Is there anyone in the town who hasn't come tonight?'

'Only one that I know of,' said the military attaché absorbedly. Lushington heard the button unfasten with a click. The Major gave a sigh of deep relief, straightened his tunic, and emerged from behind the chair. Lushington said:

'Who is that? Who hasn't come?'

'A fellow I got into conversation with in the lounge of your hotel. He seemed not to have had an invitation. In fact he asked me if he could come with me and get in on mine. He said he was a count. Bobel or some such name. Ever heard of him? He seemed a bit of an outsider.'

'I seem to have heard the name.'

'You have?'

'Somewhere or other. I don't know.'

'Well, I mean socially he may be an A1 lad and all that, but you just can't go about doing that sort of thing. I mean it's all wrong. You'd think a fellow would see that.'

'Absolutely wrong. A fellow like that needs snubbing.'

'I snubbed him all right. Don't you worry. He got his snub.'

'I'm delighted to hear it.'

At that moment a diversion was caused by the belated entry of the French diplomatic representatives, a remarkable quartette consisting of the Minister, a Charley Chaplin-like little man with the pointed beard of the stage Frenchman, round-shouldered with the weight of the *légion d'honneur* round his neck, and glancing nervously at his wife, whose immense proportions seemed as if they might at any moment evade the neo-classic creation she was wearing. Behind her came the secretary, the second-empire Baron who had recently had so narrow an escape at the hands of the Deputy-Chief of the Air Force, and beside him their military attaché in a uniform of remarkable shape and elastic-sided boots on to the heel of which spurs had been screwed. Ushers shepherded this cortège to the President's throne, and when Lushington turned round again he found that the Major was now talking to the American and Japanese Ministers. The former of these plenipotentiaries was saying:

'No, sir, I do not. The tongue of Shakespeare and *The Saturday Evening Post* is good enough for us and you can take it from me, Colonel—and you, Viscount, you bear this in mind too—if people are worth talking to they talk *English.*'

Lushington moved away through the crowd. He wondered why he had not yet seen Ortrud, because it was late in the evening and he knew that she was coming to the ball. That night in his bath he had begun to realise that he was going away and would never see her again. The thought of this disturbed and frightened him. He was going away. He would not see her again. Passing the buffet he saw General Kuno, very spick and span, wearing the riband of a recently conferred order across his chest. He and Lushington bowed to each other and as conversation was impossible went through some amicable dumb-show, beginning by Lushington offering the General a cigarette, which was accepted, and ending with the General offering Lushington a sandwich from the buffet, which was refused. Waldemar was fussing about behind the General and, in his capacity of A.D.C., wore heavy gold aiguillettes which he continually trailed into the ices and drinks of those standing anywhere near him. He kept on adjusting his pince-nez and bowing to people who came up to speak to the General. Lushington said to him:

'How are you enjoying your new job?'

'I am worried. Worried. I will tell you a secret. It is a great shame. It is no joke. Almost I am ashamed to tell you.'

'I must know the worst.'

'The armour round the room. It comes from the National Theatre. It is not genuine armour.'

'Why not?'

'It is false. A mere trick. I would tell no other stranger but you. I am angry with my country. But the committee insisted that it should be so. They were very adamant.'

'But this is the invariable practice in all countries. The use of stage properties on such occasions as these.'

'You astonish me!'

'I assure you.'

'I am much relieved.'

'But don't tell Cortney. He had better not know.'

'You are right. Above all not Mr. Cortney. It must at all costs be kept from him.'

The waltz ended and Lushington saw Da Costa hand back Mrs. Bellamy, with whom he had been dancing, to her husband. There was some clapping, but the band did not play an encore. Instead there was a pause and some picked dancers began to form up for the mazurka. Da Costa stood talking to the Bellamys for a few seconds and then made his way round the wall to the place where Lushington was. He looked hot.

'Very exhausting, this sort of thing,' he said.

'How long will it go on?'

'Until about breakfast time tomorrow. It gets more amusing later in the evening when the diplomats from the larger countries have gone away. Last year the Bulgarian consul-general did some awfully clever conjuring tricks in the Hall of the Grand Masters. Unfortunately he broke one of the clocks on the mantelpiece and there was rather a row because it turned out to be valuable.'

'Was he the man who said, "May I join this little circle of rose-buds?" when he sat on the sofa between Mrs. Bellamy, Madame Theviot and Baroness Puckler the other night?'

'That's the one. He hasn't been asked this year. It's rather a shame really. But he has no sense of proportion.'

The band had begun to play again and the dancers moved towards each other in the opening movements of the mazurka. This dance was the high-water mark of the evening. As soon as it had taken place people would begin to slip away to bed, unless they had decided to make a night of it. General Kuno was watching the mazurka beside the President, and Waldemar, left to himself for a few moments, came up to them, leading a girl by the arm. He said: 'Let me present my fiancée or, as you say in English, my sweetheart. This English gentleman is Mr. Da Costa and this English gentleman is Mr. Lushington, Hedwig.'

Hedwig was a sensible-looking girl dressed in brown velvet and like Waldemar she wore pince-nez. Lushington shook hands and was about to ask her for the first dance after the mazurka was over when, seeing Ortrud across the room, he slipped away and left this duty to Da Costa. He moved with difficulty round the crowded floor, getting caught up in evening dresses and tripping over spurs. Once he nearly upset one of the suits of armour. As he made his way round he watched her, still thinking how he would soon see her for the last time. Ortrud was talking to two men, one of them a Swedish officer who held tucked under his arm a cocked hat with yellow plumes and the other the German first secretary, an ex-flying ace, whose evening clothes were plastered with crosses in black and white enamel. These men stood by her in the clockwork, angular attitudes required of Teutonic gallantry. Lushington watched her. She was dressed in black, too dramatically, but suiting her style and figure. Once again, as on the boat when he had first seen her, he thought of Lucy. But Ortrud was taller, thinner, and her features were less subtle. Now as he looked at her she seemed like a sleek cat. He saw her straighten the gold lace that had become disarranged on the Swede's epaulette. As she did this her face did not alter, but he felt angry that she should touch another man in this way. He pushed on through the crowd. She saw him and nodded, still talking to the Swede. Lushington waited by the wall, glancing at the mazurka, which was becoming now more complicated and breathless as its leader shouted aloud the sequence of its movements. Then he felt her touch his arm. He turned—she was standing beside him. She was in black with a white flower fastened to her dress.

'My husband is not here tonight. He said that he had a *migraine* and would not come.'

'When will you dance with me? After this?'

'Two after this.'

'Two? Why not at once? After all, this is almost the last time I shall see you.'

'I know; but I have two duty dances. You understand?'

'No.'

'Is it to be one of the nights when we quarrel.'

'I hope not.'

She smiled at him, making him think that perhaps he would give up his job on the paper and try to find a post on the spot, a waiter's or something of the sort where it would not be necessary to learn much of the language. Anything so long as he could stay with her. They moved towards the doors of the ballroom. The mazurka clattered and stamped behind them. Its leader had allowed the

dancers to get more than a little out of control and he himself began to shout more shrilly than ever. He was an old
man with white dundreary whiskers and he was so thin
and shrunken that if any of the dancers had collided with
him he might have cracked in half.

Ortrud and Lushington went up the stairs. On one of
the landings they turned into an alcove and sat down under
the picture of a Swedish king, some benefactor of the
knights, in a wig and with Roman armour fitting into the
contours of his highly developed figure and wearing round
his neck the Order of the Seraphim. They sat there and
watched people passing up and down the stairs. Da Costa
appeared, half-running, behind the daughters of the Dutch
Minister. He was taking these girls towards the buffet and
all three of them were laughing a good deal. As he went
by he shouted:

'Let me warn you that someone has poured vodka into
one of the jugs of claret cup.'

He went off in pursuit of his two yellow-haired
débutantes, shaking with laughter. Ortrud said:

'So you are going to leave me and go back to England?'

'We talked of that before. Don't let's talk about it again.
What else can I do?'

'Will you be sorry that you are not going to see me any
more?'

'Don't be silly.'

'You will go back to your English miss.'

'She is not a miss and hasn't been for some time.'

In the ballroom the mazurka came to an end and there
was a great deal of clapping. They heard the Master of
the Ceremonies making a short speech. People began to
come through the doors in a stream. The American
Minister passed the alcove and, pausing for a moment to
point his finger in the shape of a revolver at Ortrud, said:

'Bang!' and walked with great deliberation down the stairs. Baroness Puckler went by with Countess Arnhfeldt and, smiling at them, went up towards the Hall of the Grand Masters. Ortrud said:

'Will you ever come back?'

'Of course I shall.'

'My lover, you are going away. You are going to leave me. What shall I do? I have only been happy with you. And now you are going away.'

'Why don't you come with me?'

'You know that I cannot. And you know that you do not want me to. It is you who are to blame for going away. You are treating me shamefully. I shall be annoying tonight. I shall annoy you. There will be time to make it up before you go. I shall come down then to the ship and wish you good-bye very nicely.'

'All right.'

'The girl you are going back to? Are you in love with her?'

'You will annoy me if you start all that again.'

'You are in love with her, then?'

'Must we have all this over again?'

'You mean that it does not matter? Because you are going away from me in any case? Do you mean that?'

'If you like.'

'I shall take another lover.'

'Oh?'

'That nice young Spaniard.'

'Yes?'

'Spaniards are better lovers than Englishmen. Did you know that?'

'I feel sure they are.'

'Am I annoying you?'

'Yes.'

The American Minister came up the stairs again, slowly, and with one hand on the banisters. He pointed his finger at Ortrud and saying 'Pop!' disappeared into the ballroom. Waldemar passed them with his fiancée on his arm. In the distance Lushington could hear Da Costa's neighing laugh. In the ballroom the band began to play *Weine nicht, mein liebe, weine nicht* in a sudden burst of sound, a musical caucus race, the result of refreshments, in which each player began where he wished and went as far as he judged suitable. Ortrud rested her hand on his knee.

'What are you thinking?' she said.

'Let's go and try some of this famous claret cup?'

'No. I have to dance with General Kuno.'

'At once?'

'Yes.'

'Blast General Kuno to hell. I hope he is blown up by some of those old school chums of his who are always trying to get him. Why should he want to dance with you at this moment? Get rid of him as soon as you can.'

More and yet more curious sounds echoed through the building from the direction of the band. Lushington went down with her as far as the ballroom, where they found General Kuno twisting his moustache and grinning fiercely like the villain in a melodrama. Lushington watched them dance away together into the middle of the crowd and then turned again towards the refreshment room. He found Cortney and Da Costa standing by the table, smoking. Cortney held out his cigarette case:

'Have a Lucky?' he said. 'Isn't this party great? It takes you back somehow. The pictures, the armour, the old panelling. Even the dresses and the uniforms. Why, we might be at the court of Catherine the Great or the *Roi Soleil*. Don't you get me, Lushington? See how I mean?'

'This sandwich takes me back even farther than the armour.'

Da Costa said: 'You've done nothing but grumble ever since you came out here. Besides, that joke is in very poor taste and not really at all funny. All the sandwiches I have eaten seemed to me very good, though I don't know why they had put caraway seeds in one of them. But with you nothing is ever right. Either Pope is annoying you or it is too hot indoors, or too cold out of doors, or your skis have come off, or the food has upset you. I should think you will be thankful to get back to England. As a matter of fact I shan't be sorry to get back there myself soon. I'm getting rather tired of this sort of thing. After all, life must have something more to offer than a series of waltzes with Mrs. Bellamy, Frau Kuno and Waldemar's fiancée. I couldn't have been sent into the world for that.'

'Oh, I don't know. I should think probably you were.'

Cortney said: 'Well, I think you are a pair of grouchers and I'm off to find Frau Mavrin and take a dance with her.'

Lushington said: 'You won't manage it, because she's booked up for the rest of the evening.'

But Cortney did not hear this and he went away from the refreshments. Lushington and Da Costa followed behind him to the ballroom. The floor was clearer now. Waldemar and his fiancée were among the couples dancing. They saw Waldemar's lips moving as he passed, counting to himself:

'*One*-two-three, *two*-two-three, *three*-two-three, *four*-two-three.'

Da Costa said: 'I am serious this time. I have done as much of this sort of thing as I can stand. I am going to resign and arrange to go out on an archæological expedition. Anyway it would be a change.'

'I should.'

'There's an oppressive feeling in the air tonight. I am tired of all these people. I shall be glad to get home to bed.'

'So shall I,' said Lushington. But he knew that he was not speaking the truth.

The dance seemed to go on for ever with endless encores and the one that followed it was equally drawn out, while Ortrud danced with the Chancellor of the University, a fat old man, who held her at arm's length while he walked round the room. Lushington danced with Baroness Puckler, who was enjoying herself a good deal and was full of stories of what the British Ambassador had said in 1903 when he had met one of the secretaries walking down Unter den Linden in brown boots. She said:

'But it is so sad that you are leaving us. I do not know what Ortrud will do. It is very necessary for a young married woman to have someone to take her about. More especially when her husband is a clever man who has important national work to perform. It is very necessary for his sake that she should be kept contented. Cannot you stay for that reason?'

'I wish that I could.'

'You must stay. We all wish it. Cannot it be arranged?'

The band boomed on aimlessly and it was late before he managed to see Ortrud again. They danced once round the room and then went upstairs to the alcove where they had sat before. That night she was in one of her moods. They sat there in silence watching the people passing up and down the stairs. The air was heavy with the scent of women's make-up and the animal smell of the men, sweating into their thick uniforms. Soon the ball would be finished and they would be going back to their homes again and another of the times when he was with her would be over, the few times that still remained to him.

People had been leaving steadily since the mazurka and now the House of the Knights was becoming quite deserted. All around him was the used-up atmosphere of the end of a party. Then the band began to pack up. Da Costa came up the stairs. He saw Lushington and Ortrud and said:

'I'm off now. Can I take you back?'

Ortrud said: 'Yes, it would be nice.'

'I'll get my coat, then, and find a drosky,' Da Costa said. He went away down the stairs.

Lushington said: 'Why am I not to take you back tonight?'

'No. Not tonight. I am in bad mood tonight. We will meet again before you go.'

'You certainly are in bad mood tonight.'

'You must not mind. I just do not want you to come back with me tonight. I would rather go with him. He will talk all the time and I shall not have to answer. I am tired and I want to get away from here soon.'

'All right.'

'Wait a moment,' she said. Very quickly she took the flower from where it was pinned to her dress and put it into his hand. He took it, not knowing at first what she had given him.

'For me?'

'Yes,' she said. 'For you.'

Da Costa reappeared. He said:

'I have got a cab. Can I take you too? Or do you want more gaiety?'

'No, I go in the opposite direction. Anyway, I would like to walk some of the way, I think.'

Da Costa said: 'The cloakroom here is a disgrace. I handed in my ticket and the attendant gave me a plumed helmet and a sky-blue cloak. I have got my own hat and

164

coat at last, but my goloshes seem gone for good, so we may be delayed a few minutes in getting away because goloshes are things that you cannot buy more than once in a lifetime.'

Lushington said: 'I shall go now, then. Good-night. Good-night.'

'Good-night,' they said.

He went down the stairs. Putting his hand in his trouser pocket he felt the flower that she had given him.

31

THE hard blue night, dissolving now patchily in the sky behind banks of cloud, was clear under the street-lamps and Lushington went through the snow, piled up on either side of the steps and archways of the High Town. There had been a light fall less than an hour before so that some of the steps were slippery and the snow balled on the soles of his shoes. Two or three soldiers staggered past, drunk early or returning from drinking late, and one of them shouted after him and half-heartedly threw some snow. In the distance he heard the noise of firing, carried through the empty streets across the town from the barracks, or perhaps from among the islands along the shore where a gunboat might be scuffling with smugglers. But he did not trouble to make up his mind which of these it was most likely to be because he was thinking of Ortrud, and how it would feel to see her no more when he was back in England, and what he would say to her when he saw her soon again to say good-bye.

A few lorries had already begun to appear in the streets and one or two of the shops were beginning to take down their shutters, but the town was still very silent. The lorries churned up the slush and made a noise with their gears as they came up the steep streets. Somewhere near-by men were shouting in a confused way as if they were calling papers. A few cars and droskies passed and the street-lamps caught the decorations and polished buttons of guests returning from the ball. The walk back seemed interminable, or rather it took place in the course of one of those passages of time that seem indefinitely extended and during which the destination approaches no nearer although more and more ground is covered. At last Lushington reached the hotel. With a great effort he pushed open the outside door.

In the lounge the servants had begun to appear and some of them with handkerchiefs tied over their heads were sweeping the floor with handleless brooms and talking to each other in shrill voices that jarred against the thin atmosphere of morning. Flosshilde had not yet arrived at her desk in the hall. Nor had the lift boy appeared, and for some reason the gates of the lift were locked, so Lushington walked up the stairs slowly and across the landings lit only by nightlights. He reached his room, took off his overcoat, and began to undress, throwing all his clothes on the floor. He was tired but with all the uneasy wakefulness of what he had come from, so that when he fell asleep, which was immediately, it was into a hagridden trance like sitting up at night in a railway carriage when burning pains run suddenly through the body and cold alternates with stifling heat. His clothes lay in a heap beside the bed.

He embarked at once on to a scene of nightmare, as if he had walked into a room not before entered that evening. It was a complicated, noisy affair, all bright colours and people moving quickly about and talking a great deal. Once he felt that he was falling through space. Through the conversations and strident musical instruments of his dream he could still hear the gurglings and detonations made by the room's radiators, hydraulic disturbances which always took place at this time in the morning.

32

IT seemed almost at once that the telephone bell rang, at
first in his nightmare, and then, becoming more conscious
of the dryness in his throat and actuality, he got out of bed
and went into the sitting-room, falling over the great-coat
lying on the floor and banging into chairs. He did not turn
on the light but, groping, blundered about the room until
he found the receiver.

'Hullo?'

'It's Pope, sir. Pope.'

'What do you want? When is it? Why haven't I been
called?'

'There's been an accident, sir. Mr. Da Costa.'

'An accident?'

'Yes, sir. An accident. It is very serious. Can you come
round at once?'

'Come round? Now? Where? What accident?'

'Mr. Da Costa's flat, sir. It is serious. If you could come
round at once, sir?'

'But I am in bed. What is the time? When did this
happen? Is it today or tomorrow?'

At the other end of the line Pope gobbled in a kind of
ecstasy of fright and refinement, at intervals making a sort
of clucking noise as he poured strings of unconnected, in-
gratiating words into the transmitter. Lushington could
hear that Pope had his mouth pressed against the instrument
as he gasped into it, hectic with melodrama:

'I take it I can count on you to come round, sir. The matter is most urgent.'

His voice faded away before Lushington could say any more.

Lushington stood in the middle of the room and wondered what had happened to Da Costa. He felt his way to the wall and round to the electric light switch. The glare dazed him and he sat down in an arm-chair and rubbed his eyes for a few seconds. The whole room seemed to be throbbing as if the band from the House of the Knights was playing in the bedroom but with muted instruments. Then he looked at his watch. He had been in bed less than an hour. Still feeling stupid with sleep he began to put on his clothes, aimlessly dressing once more in the stiff shirt and white tie which he found on the floor. He noticed that the white waistcoat had stains of claret cup on it. Only when he was fully dressed again it occurred to him that these were not the clothes in which to begin the day, but he was too heavy-eyed to take them off and dress in something else. He picked up the overcoat from the floor and put it on as he went down the stairs.

When he arrived in the lounge the hotel had been given its usual appearance. The signs of early morning had been withdrawn. Flosshilde was now at her desk. She expressed surprise at seeing him so early and was about to begin a conversation as he passed, but, smiling discouragingly, he moved on into the street and beckoned a drosky. He got into it and gave Da Costa's address. It was not yet light. There were more people in the streets now and twice a detachment of soldiers tramped past with fixed bayonets and wearing steel helmets. The drosky crossed the railway square and drove by the immoderate, Germanic nymphs straining on their plinths under the station's architrave.

There were two gendarmes at the entrance to the block of

flats. These, stage policemen out of a knock-about farce, stopped him, shaking their heads. They stood in front of the door, grunting and intransigent, making signs that he could not go in, their expressions that of highland cattle. Lushington showed them his passport, but he had to add to it a press card and the membership voucher of a defunct London night-club before they would let him pass. He went up in the lift, working it himself, and rang the bell of the flat. There was a long wait and then Pope opened the door.

'Well?' said Lushington. 'What is wrong?'

Pope could hardly speak. He was only half dressed, and Lushington noticed that he was wearing Da Costa's dressing-gown over his shirt and trousers. He had no collar and his hair was not brushed. He fluttered with his hands.

'Mr. Da Costa, sir,' he said, 'Mr. Da Costa has been shot.'

And then Lushington saw that two more gendarmes were standing in the hall behind Pope fingering their belts and the holsters of their revolvers, dimly aware that they too were of dramatic importance in the setting of something that had taken place not long before. Lushington said:

'What do you mean?'

'Come here, sir. This way.'

They went into the sitting-room, where a lot of people were standing about and almost all of whom were talking. Waldemar, very white in the face, was there and a police captain. There was a faint smell of antiseptic like a nursing home. When Lushington came in everyone stood up and clicked their heels. Waldemar came forward and, taking Lushington by the arm, introduced him to several people, some of whom were doctors. Lushington shook hands all round. Pope stood behind, shuffling with his feet and swallowing. The blinds of the room were drawn and the electric light was on. The bedroom door was open. Pope shuffled. Waldemar made a movement with his hands. Lushington saw that they intended him to go into the bedroom. He went towards the doorway and looked through it. The people in the sitting-room went on talking, but less loudly. The blinds were drawn in the bedroom as in the sitting-room and the lights were on. Lushington stood on the threshold of the bedroom and looked into the room. Then he said:

'Is he dead?'

'He's dead, sir. Dead.'

Pope swallowed.

'But what happened?'

'He was shot, sir. Shot.'

Pope clasped the dressing-gown round him. He was very upset. Lushington stared into the room. Waldemar moved forward. He said:

'This is a grave and tragic episode. The men who have done this thing have committed an act of murder. Under the new code abolishing the death penalty they render themselves liable to a sentence of fifteen years' forced labour. When they are apprehended the law will most surely exert its full rigour.'

Lushington stood and looked through the doorway of the bedroom. Here then was that rather astonishing mystery about which so much had been said that, when the fact itself was there, no further comment was possible. For the moment no near-at-hand formula seemed at all adequate. This was something well-defined and at the same time not easy to believe in. It seemed absurd, overdone. Lacking in proportion, like other people's love affairs. Here were all the signs of a loss of control. A breakdown of the essential machinery. The sort of thing no one could be expected to be on the look-out for. He rested one of his hands on the side of the door. He did not turn to hear what Waldemar was saying. The smell of disinfectant, he noticed, came from the bedroom. In the room behind him the hum of enquiring talk continued. Pope said:

'That was the only covering I could find that was extensive enough in size.'

'I see.'

'I was about to search for something else when you rang the bell, sir.'

'How did this happen?'

It took some time to find out the answer to this question. Waldemar told most of the story, with interruptions from Pope, who had not been present, and from one of the doctors, who understood but did not speak English. The other people in the room talked to each other in their own language or made noisy telephone calls. The atmosphere, the fumes of sweat and disinfectant, was midway between an operating theatre and a corner of the monkey house. The mauve and Venetian red cushions were all crumpled up at one end of the sofa. One of the shelves of the bookcase had collapsed and some heavy books had slid on to the floor, where they had remained in a heap. There was no blood.

The story came out by degrees. Da Costa, they said, had left the House of the Knights in a drosky. Crossing the square in front of the University a car driving away from the ball had drawn level. In this car were General Kuno, Waldemar, and two detectives. As the car was passing the drosky two men had run out from a side street and had begun to fire revolvers at General Kuno. General Kuno and his civilian bodyguard had replied with their automatics and Waldemar had drawn his sword. The gendarme on duty at the corner of the square blew his whistle and also opened fire. The two gendarmes who patrolled the street at right-angles to the square were near the operative end of it and were soon able to join in with the others. The horses drawing the drosky had run away. That was how it had happened. When they stopped the drosky they had found Da Costa dead. Waldemar said:

'Also a drunk man was seen brandishing a revolver, but after his arrest it was found to be but a cardboard pistol that they distribute at Maxim's on the nights of gala. Nevertheless he has been detained for further interrogation by the police. It is said that he is a count.'

Lushington thought about it all and while he thought about it he remembered something that up till then he had forgotten. He said:

'Was anyone else killed?'

Waldemar said: 'Alas, the lady——'

'The lady? What lady?'

'Frau Mavrin——'

'What happened to Frau Mavrin?'

Waldemar stammered. He said:

'She too is dead. She lived for a few minutes. But she died as they were taking her away.'

'Do you mean she was shot?'

'Yes, she was shot.'

'By these men?'

'Indeed.'

One of the fat men in black coats who crowded the room could not get the number he wanted on the telephone and he kept on tapping the instrument so that the bell gave out a number of little tinkling rings. Another of these men had taken down a book from the bookcase and was looking at the pictures in it. Lushington fingered his white tie, wondering dimly why he had come in evening dress to what seemed to be an inquest. The police captain had sent for the two gendarmes and was giving them instructions which he made them repeat after him, like children learning a lesson. The faces of everyone in the room were shiny and looked like badly made models in wax.

Pope said: 'Two peasant women on their way to the fruit market were wounded by the shots of these men, who are believed to have been Communists. The porter from the flats opposite came out to watch and was grazed by a bullet. That was from the guns of the General's plain-clothes men.'

Waldemar said: 'It is of great credit to the police that they were the cause of no grave casualties. None of their shots caused anyone a serious injury. They are in pursuit of the murderers and have high hopes of apprehending them.'

'Have they?'

'It is indeed certain.'

The heaviness of the room was almost insupportable. There seemed to be no air in it at all. Several of the men had not taken off their overcoats, which were damp from the fall of snow. The fat man at last had been put through to the number he wanted on the telephone and he was now giving a complicated message, spelling out most of the words. When he had finished he gave the message again, but in a different language. Waldemar was very upset. He took off his pince-nez and wiped them. He said:

'What must you think of my poor country, you with your English sense of constructive and far-sighted political philosophy. But here it is not understood to compromise. General Kuno had enemies. In England never have I heard that the chief of police is shot at. No matter how much the discontent with existing laws. But here of compromise little is known among the parties of the Left.'

Reviewing momentarily the situation, Lushington found that he was not thinking of Ortrud as dead. He was surprised to find that at present he did not think of her as that. And in the same way it hardly seemed that Da Costa, too, was dead, in spite of what he had seen and what he could see at any moment again if he went back to the door-way of the bedroom. He himself felt a little dazed and rather sick and he could only think that he had missed an eye-witness account of the thing for the paper and that now he had been given orders to come back to England things were beginning to happen out here. Besides, everyone was talking so much that it seemed useless to attempt to take in what they were saying. He tried to pull himself together and to decide upon something efficacious to say or to do. The first flush of excitement was dying down among the others and Waldemar was returning to his normal state of mild embarrassment. Lushington said to him:

'I am so sorry. I haven't congratulated you on your own escape yet.'

'Thank you, thank you.'

'And General Kuno.'

'I will bear your congratulations to him. It shall be done at once.'

'And the legation? Do they know there yet?'

Pope said: 'Mr. Bellamy is on his way here. I com-municated with him by telephone.'

One of the men in the room, perhaps the fat one who had been doing so much telephoning, came across to Lush-ington and began to talk to him in a language that Lushington did not understand. He talked for a long time and Lushington nodded at appropriate intervals. When the man had finished and had gone away to talk to someone else Lushington said:

'Is it light outside yet?'

He seemed to have been in the room so long that he wondered if it was late afternoon. Pope heard him and walked quickly across the room holding the dressing-gown round him like a mannequin displaying a dress. With one hand he held the dressing-gown round him and with the other he pulled the curtains aside from the window, but the door-bell rang before he had time to put out the lamps and he went to open the door while the sunlight came in through the double panes, into the room which was already filled with a yellow glow. Outside, although the sun had scarcely risen, some rays of its light caught the gilt domes of the Russian cathedral and with their coruscations accentuated the chill that was in the morning air. There were splashes of light now all over the harbour. A lot of people were moving about among the docks and several of the smaller boats were puffing up clouds of black smoke. In the streets officers carrying black portfolios under their arms were walking along to the Ministry of Defence, and boy and girl students in peaked caps were starting off for the University. Lushington thought that although he was tired it would be no good going to bed again that day. He would soon have to get some fresh air, he thought. He took a handkerchief from his pocket to blow his nose and some petals of a flower dropped on to the carpet. He sat down on a chair and began to pick them up one by one.

33

LUSHINGTON was doing his packing. The sitting-room was filled with his clothes and objects of little value acquired during his visit, none of which would fit into the available boxes. Cortney, who was helping with advice, pushed away the larger suitcase from the arm-chair and sat down. He fingered his moustache thoughtfully. The Baltic sunlight streamed in through the window. Cortney said:

"Well, you'll be glad to get back. Away from all this trouble and turmoil. Back to quiet old England where the trees will soon be getting green again. I know how you'll be feeling about it.'

'Do you?'

'You bet I do. We've all of us had to face a deal of trouble out here and you most of all. There were two persons, young, promising, handsome, socially exclusive, aristocrats in the best sense. And now they are gone. Did you ever know either of them say an unkind word, do a dishonest action, or behave in any way meanly, pettily or so that you might be ashamed of them? I think, Lushington, that you did not. It's the passing of such as these that makes me think "See here, Cortney, what will you have to say for yourself the day you come to hand in your checks? How will it feel when the Recording Angel calls your bluff for the last time?" How many of us will make the grade? It's a question that I am not man enough to answer, and I think, Lushington, that you'll say with me that you are not man enough to face up to that question either.'

Lushington, who had been straining to shut the fastenings of the bag he had been packing, gave it up, took some of the things out and began to pack another one. Litter of all kinds covered the floor. There was just room for him to kneel down while he packed. He said:

'Do you mind getting up for a moment? I think you are sitting on my stiff shirts. Or rather, what the laundry have left of them.'

'Scherbatcheff, he's gone too. The poor old Count. He's gone to rest with his ancestors. Well, perhaps he's better where he is. He's gone where count and commoner are all the same.'

'I shall miss him on the voyage back.'

'What is it, Lushington, that makes you travel by sea when you could do the journey in half the time and three times the comfort by land?'

'I thought the sea journey might make a story for my paper.'

'I daresay you're right. I love the sea myself. We Anglo-Saxon races have it just naturally in our blood. I often think I should like to be buried at sea when I have to make my reckoning with the Old Man with the Scythe. That strange old guy who gets us all in the end.'

Pope, who was in the deepest black, appeared silently in the room. He watched Lushington kneeling before the suitcase. He looked more wistful than ever. He said:

'If you wish, sir, I can complete your packing.'

'No, thanks. I prefer to do it myself.'

'I think you would be wiser to allow me to complete it, sir. I have great experience of packing. My late master, sir, poor Mr. Da Costa, often used to compliment me on my packing. He used to say that he knew no one like me. He didn't really. I hope that now that I am going to Mr. Cortney he will find me equally satisfactory.'

Cortney said: 'Pope, I am a reserved man. I come of a reserved family. We don't let our tongues run away with us. We leave most of the talking to our women folk. But at least I'll say this. If I can rely on you to serve me with the respect, the rectitude, the integrity, and the devotion that you were accustomed to accord to Mr. Da Costa I think that neither of us will have any cause for regrets.'

Cortney rose and taking his hat and stick from the bedroom, where they had been put in case Lushington should pack them, went towards the door. Pope inclined his head. Cortney said:

'So long, Lushington. I shall next see you on the quayside.'

'So long.'

Pope said: 'I was in the next room, sir, and I could not help overhearing that Mr. Cortney was speaking about death. When I was in the War, sir, of course one had to be prepared for it at any moment. My duty often took me within a few miles of the front line and a stray shell might easily have got me. But then we soldiers knew that such things were all in the day's work. We got used to it. We even used to joke about such things. I often look back on those days almost with regret. But then I was popular in the Army. I don't know how it was. The men seemed to look up to me, somehow. There are one or two experiences I should especially like to tell you, sir, as you'll be leaving this country soon and I may not have another opportunity.'

34

THE boat sailed late, after dinner, and it was dark and cold down by the docks. Lushington leaned over the side and talked to Waldemar and Cortney, who had come to see him off. Pope was there too, carrying a walking-stick with a heavy coloured-glass knob and he wore an unusually wide-brimmed black hat. He had been running about quickly, giving orders to porters, and for a few minutes he confused everybody so much that all Lushington's heavier luggage was taken on to a cargo boat bound for Stettin. However, it was recovered without much difficulty. Now Pope stood in the background leaning on his stick. When Lushington tipped him he had said, *'A bientôt,* sir,' which made Lushington wonder whether he had given him enough. The quayside was deserted except for a few loafers and some soldiers and gendarmes, watching to prevent anyone from committing a nuisance or blowing up the docks. A strong wind was blowing inland from the sea. They talked to each other awkwardly as they had been dining together and topics for conversation had run out earlier in the evening. At last a party of nondescript characters, supers from a tableau of haulers on the Volga, removed the gangway laboriously. The steam hooter sounded and a minor official in a peaked cap wound a hunting horn.

'Cheerioh, Mr. Lushington!' Waldemar shouted and saluted.

Cortney took off his hat and raised his arm in the fascist salute. In the background Pope brandished his stick.

The boat began to move away from the side, and down the watercourse. Lushington took off his hat and waved it. Waldemar and Cortney remained at their respective salutes. It was so dark that they and Pope were soon out of sight and the boat, zigzagging, passed on through the wharfs. There were cranes and low warehouses on either side and lighted flares at intervals which showed up the red and yellow wood of the buildings. On one of the quays three drunk night-watchmen were dancing hand in hand round a fire. The boat went on past a fort and from here the harbour widened into open sea. This was the last outpost of the unreal city and, prodigally dramatic, a soldier was standing on one of the bastions of the central tower leaning on his rifle, humped out by his helmet and pack into a gargoyle against the snowy castellations and pale stars. It was the final and rather masterly shot of the reel.

The night air was very cold. This ship was smaller than the one on which Lushington had come out. It was little more than a cargo boat, but there were half a dozen cabins that opened on to the dining-saloon. Lushington decided to go below and have another look at the poky smoking-room. He wondered if his brain would ever work again or if he would be obsessed for ever by the thoughts that he was thinking then.

In the smoking-room a fat man was sitting with his back to the door, sorting packages which he had taken from a gladstone bag. When Lushington came in the man turned round. It was Count Bobel.

'Hullo,' Lushington said.

Count Bobel did not get up nor remove the cigarette from his mouth. He continued to arrange his samples. He said:

'Mr. Lushington, *mon cher,* I was delighted to see your name on the list of passengers and I have persuaded the

Captain, who is a self-willed and somewhat disagreeable man, to allow you to share my cabin. He made difficulties, but at last he consented and your effects have been removed there. In that way we can converse and thereby the voyage will have less *ennui.*'

'Are we the only passengers?'

'We are the only two. How fortunate that we should be already acquainted.'

Lushington stood and watched Count Bobel arranging his brown-paper parcels. The smoke from the amber cigarette swept upwards and into his left eye. He said:

'Are you going to England this time?'

'Yes, yes. I begin with the towns of the North. Sheffield, Halifax, Bradford. Later you must give me all the *addresses* that you know in these towns. But there will be time for you to do that when we come nearer to England. My friend, what tragedies we have been through in the past weeks! What escapes! Do you know that for three hours or more I was in the hands of the police? They questioned me, *ces sales types là,* and all because I happened to be passing by when the tragedy took place. It is scarcely believable. And indeed you can well imagine how shaken were my nerves by the firing alone, without any of the police interrogation that followed. But these small nations are always *comme ça.* They find a man of the world like myself and immediately suppose that he is a revolutionary. *C'est rigolo.* And poor Madame Mavrin! Do you remember how she was our companion on the outwards voyage?'

'Yes.'

'You must know that I always thought that Madame Mavrin was attracted to you. A little *béguin*? No? Perhaps not then. But such is a thing that we men must always be on the look-out for, because how much easier it is if a woman is already half won. You especially should be on the look-out, Mr. Lushington. You have a way with women. The Princess Varvara often spoke of you after our visit to your hotel. Ah, what a humorous occasion that was. How much I have laughed over it since. You are a lucky man. I myself must not grumble. I had my share of romance. *Une jeune fille très comme il faut.* But I forget. You know her. The little reception clerk at your big hotel. And she was called Flosshilde, which is so pretty a name, more especially for me for whom Wagner will always be the supreme *maestro*. You remember her, yes? At the desk of your hotel?'

'Yes.'

'Alas,' said Count Bobel. 'Alas, the poor girl finds herself in a very difficult position. Very difficult. But she is a clever girl and no doubt she will find a way out. For my part I put such difficulties from my mind. A good friend of mine, a Brazilian, once told me that the rich men in his country, when they smoke a cigar, take only the first two or three puffs. Then they throw the cigar away. Those puffs are the best and when they want more they can buy another cigar. Sometimes I think that it is good to be with girls as my friend was with his cigars. It is the sentimental who do most harm in this world of ours. You are no doubt familiar with the works of Nietzsche? You are? I thought so. And besides, I did not forget that this girl of whom I speak was fiancée to that charming compatriot of yours whose name I cannot recall.'

35

WHEN they looked through the port-holes the next morning the snow was drifting down on to the sea. It was rough all the time on the voyage home. Lushington lay on his face in his bunk with one arm hanging down at the side and his hand touching the floor of the cabin. When he thought at all he thought about Ortrud who had been shot and Da Costa who had been shot and Lucy who had not been shot and whom, if he did not die of sea-sickness, he was soon to see again. Count Bobel, who was at that moment smoking one of his amber cigarettes, said:

'I should like some day to go to Corsica. I have seen some of the women of Corsica. They are splendid women. I should like to go to a public house in Corsica.'

'There are no public-houses in Corsica. It is like France in that respect. No public-houses and no Virginian cigarettes.'

'A public house. *Une maison close.* You understand me, yes? It is in the women of that island that I am interested.'

The boat heaved very slowly, climbing with great deliberation up one side of a wave. When it came to the top of the wave it paused and for a few seconds it seemed that it would remain suspended permanently on the crest of the swell. Then it came down again suddenly, moving more quickly as it began to rise once more and to approach another apex. The beams creaked. Count Bobel nearly lost his balance and, steadying himself by clutching Lushington's ankle, said:

'If one had enough money, that is to say if one was successful enough at one's business, which is really the same thing, it would be pleasant to make a trip with the object of ascertaining the relative beauty of the women of Europe. For my part I like young girls. *Les jeunes filles en fleur*. To me they seem more fresh. There are others who think differently. I know men who will speak only of the mature woman as a possible mate. They wish for experience, sophistication, in a word the *femme du monde*. But to me there is but slight beauty in such a one. Little romance.'

Lushington, musing on those fields of asphodel through which he felt that he might soon be wandering, turned over on his back and swallowed. Very slowly the waters beneath raised his bunk at an angle so that he could watch through the port-hole the greenness of the sea and the creamy foam driving along the crest of the waves. Drops of water coursed interminably down the thick glass of the port-hole. The boat's engines sounded only faintly, like the distant buzzing of bees. Here too there was a smell of cocoanut oil. Count Bobel said:

'There is one method and one alone of avoiding sea-sickness. Always I employ it. You wind this material round the waist. There is a great deal of this material and always you wind it round the waist. It has the effect of keeping the internal organs of the body in a position of constancy. The more tight you can bear it, the more effective is this remedy. Can I draw your attention to this method of avoiding sea-sickness, Mr. Lushington? I would be glad indeed to wind it round for you myself. Sea-sickness is a most distressing malady. Once I can remember many years ago it happened that I was *en touriste* at Nice and I had invited a young lady to accompany me on a trip in a motor-boat. She had one of those very full figures that have in these days gone out of fashion to some extent. Her very fair hair went well with her style of dress. She was a remarkable girl in her way and very attached to me. I remember for example how much she was looking forward to the trip. Then as soon as she got out to sea she began to complain that she was feeling unwell. It was no use my telling her that the whole thing was her imagination. She insisted that she felt faint. I recall how sorry I was that I had not warned her beforehand that all would have been satisfactory if she had taken the the very simple precaution of wrapping round her just a few yards of the material that I have here. In that way all would have been well. The delicate machinery of the body would have been kept in place. There would have been none of the unpleasantness that followed. I was sorry because the girl was genuinely attached to me. I tell you this story about myself only because it occurs to me that you might profit by this simple contrivance.'

Count Bobel dropped the stub of his amber cigarette on the floor and stamped on it with his foot. He wore shoes made of imitation snake skin and with patent-leather toe-caps. The wind passed quickly along the sides of the ship and made a whistling noise through the cracks of the port-hole. The beam in the cabin next door creaked continuously. Lushington sat up in the bunk, supporting himself by holding on to the curtain at the side. Count Bobel retreated slightly. He said:

'In Russia we have an expression—*nitchevo*. It is difficult to render into another language. It is in reality untranslatable. It means *nothing* or, more freely, *what does it matter*? It is a very popular expression, characteristic, in a way, of our people. I tell you this because I think this is a moment when such a philosophy of life might be of value to you. Say to yourself—*nitchevo.*'

It was rough all that day and all the next one too. Owing to bad weather they were almost twelve hours longer on the sea than the scheduled time.

36

LUSHINGTON went along the stone passages into which the sun never penetrated. They had told him downstairs that there was a new literary editor. He waited, talking to Miss Arnold in the outer office, while the new literary editor finished some stuff. Then he went in. The new literary editor, who looked if possible more shifty than the last one, said:

'Who did you say you were? Yes, I remember your name. Didn't you go off somewhere? I can believe you it was cold. Wasn't there a row? Someone got shot or something? Booth was talking about it. Were you in on that? No, you missed it. Well, these things will happen, but all the same an eye-witness account is the only thing that cuts any ice when it's a small affair like that. It brings it home to the public, you know. People feel that they can get their teeth into it. Of course, in the old days there'd have been a terrible to-do about that young chap. *Civis Romanus sum* and so on. But all that's done with now, and a good thing too, I expect. I suppose you knew him well, being English and about the same age, in a small place. They shot a lady at the same time, didn't they? They did? Yes, I thought so. I saw something about it. Was she a friend of his?'

'Yes.'

'I expect you knew her too. That's the thing about a small place. You know everybody. What was she like? A nice girl?'

'Yes, she was.'

'Sad,' the literary editor said, making some marks in blue pencil on a typescript. 'Hanging's too good for fellows like that who massacre women and children. And by the way, Miss Arnold, you will find that I shall be shooting you or something of the sort if I catch you muddling up those files again. It took me half an hour yesterday to collate the material for the historical competition. It just isn't good enough. You must get that into your head. It's all a question of having a system and sticking to it. After all, it's not much to ask.'

Lushington said: 'The envelope in that pigeon-hole? It looks like my writing. May I——?'

'Anything you like, old man. It was all there when I took over. Found a treasure trove?'

'No, no. Just some stories of mine. I don't know how they can have got there. I've mislaid them for some time. I'll look through them and then perhaps you might be able to use them. Anyway, I'd like you to see them. They might do for the feature page.'

37

GOING eastwards there was a place beyond the Tower where they could sit and overlook the river. It had been Lucy's idea that they should go there. Lushington had once proposed to her on that veranda and after she had met Da Costa the three of them had been there together on several occasions. Perhaps as a sort of mourning for Da Costa she was wearing country clothes, tweeds and low heels. The place was reached with some difficulty because she had made up her mind that the way there should be an expedition, a pilgrimage, and they arrived later than they had intended. They walked through the bar and beyond it on the wooden platform. It was too cold to sit out in the open, but that was what Lucy had decided that she wanted to do. The evening was drawing in and lights were appearing along the river and on the few boats that passed by them. The water below the veranda had the slimy, viscous quality of the Thames and it seemed a denser liquid as it sucked and swelled beneath the boards. The rows of warehouses opposite, simplified by dusk, took on coherent, almost intellectual forms. In each direction these shapes ended among the mists that were drifting up from the marshes. Sometimes fog signals sounded. A Scandinavian ship, done up in cream and green paint, had been moored to the right of them. The fog signals went off three at a time. Lushington said:

'It is much too cold to have come here.'

Down-stream, on one of the larger buildings, there were

cranes jutting out with a cloud behind them that caught and held for a moment the ochre-coloured light, across which dark flights of gulls sometimes passed. A ridiculous boat like a coracle with a triangular red sail passed them and floated on with the current. There was no sign of life on the big cream-and-green Scandinavian, but three men in a dinghy with set expressions on their faces were rowing against the tide towards her. Lushington pointed to them and said:

'Look. Treasure Island.'

Lucy said: 'This woman who was killed at the same time. Was there anything between them?'

'No.'

'Are you absolutely sure?'

'Absolutely.'

'Did you know her well?'

'Quite well.'

'Was she attractive?'

'Yes.'

'You're sure he wasn't in love with her?'

'Yes.'

'What was she like?'

'Oh, I don't know. Rather sweet. She was the wife of a professor. They had only been married a few years.'

'How wretched.'

For some reason the situation seemed suddenly to have become easier. He did not know why he felt that. Before now he had not made up his mind about Ortrud. He had known what he had thought when he was on the sea, but there such feelings might have had their origin in being on the sea. But now it all seemed very clear. Lucy said:

'Now there are only us.'

And at once, not leaving any time for him to answer, she said:

'From what you say it must all have looked rather like this?'

'Do you remember when we saw the ships through the trees as if they were growing in the field?'

'Was it like that?'

'Only less real.'

'How do you mean real?'

'I don't know exactly.'

'The people or the places?'

'Both.'

The damp came up in a strong gust from the bed of the river. More gulls dipped across the cloud. The men in the dinghy had reached the ship and one of them was making passes at a rope ladder with his boat-hook. Lushington shivered. He said:

'Have another?'

'Yes.'

There were a few more people now in the saloon bar. Among them was the man who asked people their names when they came to the office and who controlled the house telephone without much success. This man saw Lushington at once and said:

'Back to the army again, sergeant?'

'That's it.'

'Seen you before down here.'

'Have you?'

'It's a nice little place. We get all sorts down here. You wouldn't believe. Artists. One of them got fifty pounds for a picture he did. I remember him well. He was down here at the time of the lightermen's strike. Used to sit out there all day. An artist, you know. Did some pictures. He got fifty pounds for one of them. That was time of the lightermen's strike. All sorts we get.'

'What will you have?'

The man stroked his face in meditation and said:

'Thanks, mine's a bitter with a drop of old in it.'

Lushington handed the man with the birthmark his drink and took his own and Lucy's. When he went outside again she was standing up and leaning her hand against one of the posts that supported the wooden roof of the veranda. She was looking across to the other side of the river where the warehouses were now almost hidden by the sallow mist. She said:

'I suppose I am more or less yours now.'

'Yes.'

'If you still want me.'

The mist was thickening and carried with it the acrid scent of fog and brought a smarting to the eyes. The cold had become intense. One of the men from the dinghy had at last succeeded in getting on board by way of the rope ladder. The other two remained in the boat, gloomily watching him. Lucy said:

'Who were you talking to in the bar?'

'The porter from my office.'

'The paper?'

'Yes.'

'Does he always come here?'

'I don't know. He said he had seen me here before.'

'I expect he thinks I'm a tart.'

'I was just wondering.'